MW00652830

the Book of Angel

ANGIE BOWEN

Tandem Light Press
950 Herrington Rd.
Suite C128
Lawrenceville, GA 30044

Copyright © 2022 by Angela Bowen

All rights reserved. No part of this book may be reproduced,
scanned, or transmitted in any printed, electronic, mechanical,
including photocopying, recording, or any information storage
and retrieval system, without permission in writing from the
publisher. Please do not participate in or encourage piracy of
copyrighted materials in violation of the author's rights.

This novel is inspired by true events. The author and publisher have
made every effort to recreate events, locales and conversations from
her memories of them. In order to maintain their anonymity, in some
instances, names of individuals and places have been changed. Some
identifying characteristics and details such as physical properties,
occupations and places of residence have also been changed.

Tandem Light Press paperback edition Spring 2022

ISBN: 978-1-7376438-7-6

PRINTED IN THE UNITED STATES OF AMERICA

CONTENTS

This book is dedicated to everyone that has impacted my life: the good ones, the bad ones, the ones I embraced, the ones I didn't, the ones that loved me, the ones that I didn't love, the ones that left, the ones that stayed.

ALL OF THEM but especially my biological family, my foster family, my adopted family, my husband, my kids, and my closest friends... 1-4-3

"*Generally, by the time you are Real, most of your hair has been loved off, and your eyes drop out, and you get loose in the joints and very shabby. But these things don't matter at all, because once you are Real, you can't be ugly, except to people who don't understand.*"

– Margaret Williams,
The Velveteen Rabbit

Content Warning: Please note that there are instances of child abuse, sexual abuse, and a suicide attempt that may be triggering or disturbing to some readers. Chapters 6 and 7 can be skipped and the events inferred from later chapters.

FOREWORD

I remember the first time I met Angie Bowen as clear as day. She was interviewing for the science teacher position on the seventh-grade team on which I taught. I asked her what made her think she wanted to teach seventh graders and she replied that they were her favorite. I knew right then and there that a lasting friendship was in the making. Our friendship has since turned in to an older and younger sister relationship. Angie began sharing parts of her childhood experiences with me and I easily saw why she was so empathetic with many students. I told her many times she needed to share her life stories with some of the students, but she hesitated. Rightly so; she knew it might change the student's perspective of her to the student if she shared.

Twenty years later, the time has come for her to share her story. Angie has written a novel for all times. The story of Angel is a touching story of how a little girl persevered and used faith, hope, and love to become the woman she is today. An angel and a rabbit are the glue that hold Angel together. The message 1-4-3 became her silent code for her family and friends. In this time of uncertainty and unrest, I hope her story can bring peace.

Sincerely,
Robin Krause
1-4-3

PREFACE

ONE DAY IN high school, one of my favorite teachers said that I was a good writer. I never really thought I was a good writer.

One day, my foster mother told me I was a good story-teller. I didn't think I was that good.

One day, my professor in college told me that I had a great story that I should share with others. I didn't think my story was shareable.

One day, one of my colleagues told me that I should write a book about my story because I wrote things well, I could tell stories, and my life story was inspirational.

So, I thought, *well maybe I might could do that.*

One day, my son and daughter said that I should definitely write a book.

One day, two years ago, I wrote the book.

The power of encouragement never stops; the power of a word is like a seed that keeps growing forever.

1-4-3 is code for "I Love You," and God does love you.

So do I, and so do so many people that you may or may not have met yet.

My prayer for you is when you read this book, you will realize that.

ACKNOWLEDGMENTS

FAMMY AND STEVEN: Without you two, I wouldn't be here. People usually don't acknowledge people that have hurt them, but without those experiences, I would not have a book to dedicate. You are both somewhere else now. I do believe there was good in you, and you did all you knew to do. Thank you for giving me life.

My biological sister and brother: I don't know if I ever told you how incredibly thankful I am for what you guys did for me growing up. I am so proud of you for making your life meaningful and inspirational to others.

To my foster family: God placed me with you, but he gave me you. Brenda and Tommy, nothing will ever repay you for what you taught me—love. Michelle, thank you for sharing your family. Tammy, you are an inspiration to me.

To Ricky and Laverne: thank you for showing me what country life is and for loving me as much as your own.

To my husband: This is about our journey and how God brought us together. You taught me how to be loved and the meaning of 1-4-3.

To my son: You saved me; you made me realize how much I can love. You are incredibly loved and chosen. As long as you are living, my baby, you will be.

To my daughter: You were prayed for, you are my best friend. You are beautiful; you are my Scoobie.

To Robin: God knew when he placed me with you that we would become sisters and friends forever. You were instrumental in helping me make this happen.

To my past teachers: don't stop believing that you are making a difference, you might be teaching someone who will one day write a book, and it might be about you.

To my friends: You, you all know who you are. You are my top 25%. Thank you for supporting me.

To Tandem Light Press: Again, God said, "Here you go, Angie," and there you guys were. That's how he works. He is the God of I am.

Finally, to the boy that called me ugly: I have never forgotten you. But because of you, many young people now know that they are never ugly and will never be. I hope you grew up and realized that words are powerful because, as in the words of the Velveteen Rabbit, "ugly is only in the eyes of the person that has never been loved."

INTRODUCTION

I WAS BORN in 1970 to a mother that immigrated from Holland and a father that had just come back from Vietnam. My mother already had my older brother and sister, and my father was dealing with his own demons.

We lived in southern California before the Internet, before rules and regulations existed for custody, and neglect and abuse were identified and addressed.

We moved around California quite often. Sometimes things were stable, but mostly we moved from home to home. We lived in apartments, sometimes in hotels, sometimes in shelters, and many times we were homeless. The term "Hobo" meant a homeless person back then, and we were, by definition, "Hoboes."

When things were good, I loved riding my bike, playing sports, and chasing my older brother around, and I loved music. My sister loved movie stars. But things weren't always good; most of the time, things were pretty bad. My mother often put us in situations where she would sell everything we had to make rent, vanish in the middle of the night, bring men home at all hours, and she and I fought, a lot.

My mother was beautiful. She was the most beautiful person I have ever seen, even to this day. She looked like

Sophia Loren, with her mother (my grandmother) born and raised in Italy. Her father (my grandfather) was German (so I have been told). Unfortunately, she had a way of getting things from men, which eventually led to horrific trauma.

My mother brought home an equally beautiful man one day, but his beauty stopped short at the surface. He was wanted by the FBI for attempted murder, kidnapping, grand theft auto, statutory rape, and numerous other charges.

This began a period of pure hell. We were subjected to horrific abuse, neglect, violence, and emotional scars that still exist for all of us. We eventually made our way from California to Georgia (where his family lived). Eventually, his past caught up with him, and we were all caught in a stolen car. We were then placed in protective custody, and for a moment in time, things were stable. However, my mother could not escape his ways, and she chose to be with him.

She loaded my sister and me up in a borrowed car, drove to a subdivision in Savannah, Georgia, opened the door, and told us to get out. She drove away, and we never saw her again for years. My sister and I were placed in an orphanage and eventually placed in foster care.

Foster care was in itself an experience, but my foster family gave me a foundation that I so desperately needed, and I graduated high school.

I became a mother at a very young age and married my high school sweetheart. Eventually, I earned a bachelor's degree in education, followed by an EdS, and have been a teacher for over twenty-five years.

This book is my story.

It is a story of a little girl that believed she wasn't loved, she believed she was ugly, and that no one wanted her. She learns through faith and her inner voice that beauty is more than appearance. It is about becoming loved and learning to love others.

Maybe her story can inspire others to know that their greatest story is yet to be told and yet to be finished.

CHAPTER 1

RABBIT HOLES

ANGEL STARED OUTSIDE her kitchen window.

She didn't know how they were getting on the porch. Her herb garden was high off the ground on her back porch, but they kept getting up there eating her herbs.

Dang rabbits.

She watched a rabbit peeking out of his hole in the yard. It was looking straight at her, as if he was saying, "Hey lady, you sure have a nice herb garden." Angel glared at the rabbit.

"Go away, rabbit!" she yelled.

Why did she think this was a good idea? Last season she'd had an issue with rats on the back porch because she had the bright idea to put a bird feeder out there. Josh had hung a bird feeder close to the porch so she could see the birds from her kitchen window. But the rats had decided to climb up the feeder and eat the bird seeds. So instead of birds, she saw big, gigantic ugly rats.

Now she was having an issue with rabbits.

All of her friends said growing an herb garden was easy. *Yeah right,* she thought. She worked all day at the start of quarantine in March to make a homemade raised flower bed garden sort of thing. She even painted a cute little sign to hang in front of it, although the sign was a little lopsided. But, oh well. She tried, right?

Dang rabbits.

Now it was May and instead of herbs growing, she had a rabbit farm. When they drove up the driveway coming home from grabbing something to eat the other night, Angel saw thousands of rabbits scatter. Literally scattered everywhere. Well, maybe not thousands, but definitely a whole lot of them.

Living in the country they always had critters, deer, even one time a pet fox that someone had dropped off, and an occasional cow that had gotten out of a pasture, but these rabbits had taken over their small farm. The rabbits built tunnels under their front yard and connected those tunnels to the back yard. Angel would swear that they probably had tunnels all the way to Atlanta.

There were holes everywhere, all over their small North Georgia farm, which was ironic to Angel because she knew a thing or two about rabbit holes. Only her rabbit holes were a little different.

She had her own secret way of going down rabbit holes. Not real rabbit holes, it was just her way of coping with stress. She could make her mind go somewhere else, and it allowed her to zone out when she got stressed. It drove Josh crazy, but it was the only way she could deal with life sometimes. She had always done it, ever since she was little. She didn't drink or smoke, tried real hard to not cuss, except when she was really angry and that was only when no one was around or when her high school students drove her crazy. Her rabbit holes were just a way of escaping reality. She couldn't really stop them when they happened, but the older she'd gotten, she'd felt the need less and less.

Dang rabbits.

Angel wondered how far those tunnels really went. Ever since they'd been quarantined, she'd noticed a lot more rabbit holes in her yard. Covid had allowed her and Josh to teach from home, and they'd done a lot lately to fix up their home. Although they built their home twenty years ago, a lifetime of late ball games for both her kids and her husband had led to some neglect of her small dream home. These rabbits weren't helping her get the house in order either.

"Josh, those rabbits ate all of my green onion stalks from my herb garden. All of them!" Angel screamed to Josh, who was inside the house in the back bedroom.

"I told you that putting a spice garden on the porch wouldn't keep them out until we screened the back porch in. Your stupid cats did a number on the screen, and we have to replace it," Josh yelled back.

Angel rolled her eyes, it wasn't a spice garden. It was an herb garden, and, well she didn't have any cats now. Those cats were long gone, and she still didn't have a replacement screen. He could replace that screen anytime. *Stupid rabbits.*

How was she going to be an herb gardener, when she couldn't keep the darn rabbits off the porch?

Angel walked outside to the back porch to figure out what to do next and her phone vibrated letting her know she had a text. She looked down at her phone and read: "He is gone," in the text from her brother.

She sat down on her back porch swing and reread it, this time time a little slower.

He is gone.

She wasn't shocked.

He was gone.

She was expecting it sometime soon.

She moved her feet to make the swing move. The same swing that had survived two kids, many dogs, crazy cats, and now some psycho rabbits that apparently liked green onions.

She stared at the text again.

Why does this text even matter to me? she thought.

It's not like he was ever in her life anyway. They tried to have a relationship. She thought it would work when her brother finally found him after searching for many years. She could still remember the day her brother called years ago with the news.

It was a moment that she had dreamed about for years. She'd thought it was going to be the moment she would finally have a fairy-tale ending. She'd thought she was going to have a real dad, a real biological parent, in her life. She rolled her eyes at the thought of that because that hadn't happened. Not by a long shot.

Her phone beeped, and Angel looked again at it. She read the next text.

"He went peacefully," it said.

What did that mean? Angel wondered.

Did it mean that he made peace with himself for not having a relationship with his daughters, that he never got to know his grandchildren, that he made things straight with his own demons, or did it mean he found peace with God? She just didn't know.

At least her brother had a relationship with him.

Her relationship with her biological dad, Steven, was far from the fairy tale ending. She tried really hard to have a relationship with him, but things were always weird between them, mostly because she just kept catching him in lies. She just didn't understand why he couldn't own up that he wasn't there for her, her sister, or her brother growing up. And why couldn't he have been there for his grandkids, her kids?

He was just like her mom. He turned out just like her. He never cared about anyone but himself. He was just like Fammy. Fammy.

She hadn't thought a whole lot of her real mother in a long, long time.

Fammy and Steven. What a couple, she thought. It was no wonder that those two ended up with each other. They were both crazy, selfish, unstable, and had so many issues with everything: drugs, alcohol, people. She never understood why both of them could just walk away from their kids.

But they did, and no amount of therapy, reasoning, or justification would ever convince her that they had a reason to do what they did.

Nothing.

Angel loved her kids. They were her whole life, literally. She would die for her kids, and anyone that knew her knew that.

Angel felt like she was a good mom. Even if she hadn't done anything else right in her life, she was a good mom, even if they're now both adults. She would have never left her kids and let her kids go through the things that she went through.

Maybe Steven was able to find a way to forgive himself.

She didn't know, and honestly, it hurt too much to think about it.

When she did start thinking about those things, she'd find a way to go into her rabbit hole, which was basically her safe place; a place for her to go in her mind where no one could touch her. She could go there and be safe.

She put her phone down and looked out in her yard with her dog in her lap. He looked back at her.

Angel wondered if he knew what she was thinking.

Wondered if that rabbit out there knew what she was thinking too?

She loved her animals and had always had a love for all animals.

Maybe not the rats though.

Josh tolerated her love for animals, but the older they'd gotten, even he began to enjoy the comfort of their two dogs. She had her little dog, Kobi and he had his big dog, Jake. It was actually the third dog named Jake they'd owned. Josh always wanted a dog named after the country song, "Feed Jake, he has been a good dog." So every dog they've had, they've named Jake. People got confused because they couldn't believe any dog could live so long, but then she'd have to explain it's actually a different dog, same name.

She looked down at Kobi, "You wouldn't ever leave Momma, would ya?" she asked him.

Kobi looked at her and cocked his head to the side as if he understood what she was saying.

Angel loved the scripture verse about animals being in heaven. There was no way God would put this sweet little dog on earth without having some sort of plan for him. Kobi was given to her by one of her high school students a couple of years ago when her other dog got killed by a wild dog that someone had dropped off in the woods. She came to school upset that morning after it happened, and one of her students surprised her a couple of weeks later with a puppy, which she ended up naming Kobi. She'd named him after Kobi Bryant, the basketball player. Angel liked Kobi Bryant because of all the things he'd done for women's basketball, and because he has a daughter that plays basketball. They have that in common.

Kobi definitely came at the right time in her life.

Angel scratched Kobi's ears and wondered how time had flown so fast. People say that all the time: "time flies."

She didn't really understand that until she'd watched her

kids graduate high school and then they were in college, and then they were gone.

Where had the time gone? She was almost fifty years old. Fifty years of her life have been lived, most of those have been spent with Josh by her side.

"Kobi, if I wasn't your mom, where would you have ended up?" She continued to scratch behind his ear.

Kobi looked at her and just stared as if he was trying to answer her.

As Angel scratched Kobi's ears, she sat on her swing and pondered at the thought of how different her life would have ended up.

How much different would her life be now?

What would her life have been if she had not lived in an orphanage or grown up in a foster home?

Would she have met her husband?

Would she have ever become a teacher?

Would she have become a mother?

"What do you think, Kobi? Do you think I would be the same as I am now?" she kept scratching his little head.

Angel just kept swinging and thinking about the text.

Life has this incredible way of working out the way it was always supposed to. She believed that with everything she had. Angel had been through some really rough moments. Maybe she was the sacrifice, like when Abraham brought Isaac to the altar, so her children wouldn't have to experience the same challenges.

She really didn't think God really worked like that, but if she did go through that so her kids wouldn't have to endure pain, then she would do it again and again.

She has seen some really bad things in her younger life, really scary things. Things that were so horrific that she would never share them. Every once in a while, she would open up to someone, but most of the time she kept them to herself.

Now that she was older, she'd realized that bad things happen all the time. Bad things happen to good people, good things happen to bad people; it's inevitable. Life is just as bad as it is good. She never thought that God picks and chooses who goes through things, people just do bad things. To Angel, the trick was to keep going, keep looking at what could be, and just keep moving toward the good. Try to see that the good things are bigger and brighter than the bad. Her whole life has been centered on trying to be something good, and if she couldn't be good, she could at least be something.

She sat in her swing and looked past the woods, past the rabbit that ran through the yard, and past the present, and looked far back into her past, and went down into her rabbit hole.

CHAPTER 2

FAMMY AND STEVEN

Fammy

THE YEAR WAS 1967, and she was so ready to leave Germany. She was tired of playing the bar scene, picking up men each night. Taking them back to her room for a quickie, and then got just enough money to live the high life for a couple of days. If she was lucky enough to find a serviceman that would keep her a while, then she could stay satisfied for a little longer. Servicemen always treated her well; they were desperate for a woman and eager to spend that money. She thought she had found one before, but he left just as soon as he discovered she was pregnant. Well, she wasn't pregnant. She just told him that to see if he would sponsor her to the States. God, she badly wanted to get to the States. She had heard about all the "far out" stuff going on in states. Of course, she didn't know what "far out" meant. She barely knew English. In Holland, where she was from, they learned English in high school. She knew just enough to get the servicemen to pay attention to her. They were so intrigued and fascinated by foreign girls.

Holland was beautiful but it was small, contained, and she had done everything she wanted to do there. But in the States, that is where things were happening. Free love, free expression. She had seen on the news where people would just load up vans and travel all around the country. She even saw where you could smoke and get drugs anywhere. Yes, that's where she wanted to be. She was young and knew that this was the prime of her life. She knew she was pretty. She was what the Dutch called "*mooie vrouw.*" People often said she resembled Sophia Loren, the actress from Italy. Just like Sophia, she had Italian in her genes.

Fammy's mother was Italian, and her father was from Germany. Fammy's mother was short and fat, like many in her family, but not Fammy. In her mind, she knew that she would not get fat like her mom, because then she would lose her biggest strength—her small petite body. That was what these servicemen liked; they wanted a limber woman, who knew her body and how to please a man. She was good at that. She worked the streets in Holland when she was younger and picked up skills that helped her earn a pretty good reputation with Germany's men. She was Fenncina Jospephina Lamein, called "Fammy" for short, and men knew her, and they knew her quite well. She was proud of her name and intended to use it tonight. She knew that all she had to do was turn her head, throw her hair around, and lick her bottom lip. Then she had them in her palm. She could get whatever she wanted. She had the looks and the body. If she could just find the one that could help her get where she wanted to go.

She grabbed her coat, looked one last time in the mirror, smiled seductively, and thought to herself, *tonight will be the night,* and shut the door.

Steven

He was tired, so tired. After serving a few weeks in Vietnam, his whole body ached, his head ached, his mind hurt. He had seen some things and had done some things that no one would ever know. He wouldn't tell them, and if he did, it would only be a made-up version. How would they know? It was his life and his experience. Nobody cared about the Vietnam vets. That was one of the many reasons why he was glad that he became stationed in Germany. He wasn't ready to go home yet. He would be expected to go to college. That might be fine for his brother, but it wasn't for him. He couldn't stand the thought of sitting in a classroom, pretending to learn. He'd enlisted in the Army to get away from his family. He had a considerably large family in Colorado with three sisters and three brothers. His parents weren't rich but not poor. They did what they could to survive. They named him Steven Douglas Pickett. He was a direct descendent to General George Pickett, who was a general in the army. He was proud of that too. General Georgie Pickett was known for Pickett's Charge. Some people said he was a traitor and failure, but he didn't think so. General Pickett had served and done his duty, and that was good enough for him.

Steven was ready to see the world. When he was in Vietnam, he and his buddies used to listen to the song. "Sittin' on the Dock of the Bay," and Steven just wanted his life to stay that way. He didn't want to go back to the States, where everything was in chaos. He could care less about politics, and that's all he saw on the news. Colorado wasn't California, but it had its share of free spirits. He didn't associate himself as one of those people gallivanting around the States as if they didn't have any responsibilities. Still, Steven wasn't someone that was going to follow the rules of the generation of the fifties either. He was just glad to be alive.

Every day someone was killed in Vietnam. He had laid awake at night and just shook with fear. He wasn't a scaredy-cat or anything, but the enemy didn't care who you were, even if you were 6'5 and weighed 250, everyone was a target. All that body just meant you were a bigger target. He was about 5'10 and weighed about 180. He was barely twenty. He knew that you did what you were told to do, and hoped you made it out alive and not in a body bag in a helicopter going home to weeping parents. The thought of his mom and dad standing over his coffin terrified him. No, he was alive and ready to pursue the next step of his life, whatever that might be. He had nowhere to be, nobody to take care of, and money in his pocket. He was lucky that he got to stay rent-free with his commander's family stationed in Germany. All he had to do was make sure that the wifey was safe. And no, he wasn't interested in her. She was a little too plain for him and way too needy. He just played with the kids and spent his nights at the bars.

Tonight, he's headed to spend some money, some energy dancing, and have a drink. Oh, how he loved to drink. If he had a weakness, it would be booze. Whiskey, scotch, beer, you name it—he loves it all. It kept him going in Vietnam, the beer. He doesn't need a woman, but he needs his beer. Maybe he'll get lucky, but all he really cared about was getting drunk.

CHAPTER 3
THE BIKE

THIS IS THE best movie ever made, Angel thought as she looked at the page in *Tiger Beat* magazine. She wanted to see it so badly, but her mom wouldn't let her. *Grease* was the name of the movie, and it was in the theater in downtown Ventura. She'd also seen it on a poster for it when they'd gone and seen *Return to Witch Mountain.* Her sister got to see it, but she couldn't. Becca only got to see it because she was invited to an all-girls slumber party and all the girls got to go the movie theater.

Angel wanted to go, but her stepdad said she had to stay with him. He said it was too mature for her. Angel assumed he was talking about "making out." Angel was eight years old, and she knew what sex was. Angel had walked in on her mom and her stepdad one time. Angel thought it was really weird to see her stepdad on top of her mom. It was gross. She rolled her eyes and continue to flip the pages of the magazine

There were a lot of pictures of movie stars in the magazine, but she liked Sean Cassidy. She thought he was pretty cute, but not like she was in love with him or anything. She heard some older girls at school talk about how they would like to make out with him. It was the first time she ever heard girls talk about that sort of thing. Mostly she overheard boys because that's all she hung out with anyway. The boys would mostly talk about sports and riding their bicycles. She did hear them talk about this girl named Missy, she was the prettiest girl in their grade. Everyone knew it, and the boys would talk about how they would love to make out with her.

They didn't talk about Angel that way. She was too tall and too fat for them. She was one of the first girls to get picked for dodgeball though, and they always let her play kickball.

The only person that ever told her she was pretty, was her stepdad, Mike, especially when he took her on fishing trips. He didn't take anyone else but her. He said it was their very special time together. Angel liked to fish but not as much as her stepdad did. She just went because he wanted her to spend time with him. Most of the time, when he did things to her during their fishing trips, she would just pretend that she was a rabbit tunneling through a hole. She liked rabbits and rabbits could dig holes really fast. So, she just would act like her mind was digging a hole.

She kept flipping through the magazine and saw a page with John Travolta, and he was super cute. She threw the magazine down. She was bored. She didn't really want to read a magazine anyway.

She wanted to go outside, play soccer and ride her bike. But the rain stopped her today, and now she was stuck in the room with her sister, who loved movies, movie stars, and *Tiger Beat*.

Angel thought her sister was obsessed with them or something. She had posters hung all over her side of the room, even on the ceiling.

Who puts posters of stupid movie stars on the ceiling? Angel thought to herself.

Becca knew every single movie they all starred in and even pretended to be them sometimes.

Angel rolled her eyes and sat up from the bed.

"Angel, you pretend to be Danny, and I will be Sandy," Becca said. "Get up in the bed and say, "summer lovin' had me a blast'."

"That's stupid, why do I want to do that? Besides, why do I always have to be the boy?" responded Angel.

"I can be the boy if you don't want to. I like being Danny," Becca said, as she stood on her bed and threw a pretend home-made microphone in Angel's hand.

"Besides your hair is short and you can jump off the bed quicker than me," Becca said to Angel.

That made Angel angry. Her Dorothy Hamill haircut was only because it made her run faster when running on the soccer field.

"My hair is short because it makes me play better, and I can kick the ball farther than anybody on my team. Dorothy is one of the best female skaters ever. She could play soccer if she wanted to. Maybe if you quit playing with Barbie dolls and movie stars, you would see that. Duh." Angel said to Becca.

Becca proceeded to stand on the bed and sing, "Met a boy cute as can be"

Angel said, "Met a girl stupid as me. Sandy is stupid!" Even though Angel really thought both Danny and Sandy made a cute couple.

"Sing it right, Angel! Sing it," Becca threw a stuffed animal at Angel in disgust.

Angel rolled her eyes and off the bed, "I'm out of here. I'm going to ride my bike."

"It's raining, and you can't!"

Angel ignored her as she stormed out of the room.

"You can just go and sit on it," yelled Becca as she threw another stuffed animal at Angel.

"You're not Fonzie, Becca!" yelled Angel back.

Angel ran outside to see if it had stopped raining, and to her delight, it had.

She ran to the garage and grabbed her bike. Why does her sister want to be a movie star anyway? She wanted to play soccer, ride her bike, and be outside. Angel was pretty happy right now and hoped that her life could stay this way. Kristine, one of her friends, just gave her an old bike because she got a new one. Angel loved it. It even had a basket on the front with a tiny plastic rabbit at the top.

Angel pedaled and made her way out of the garage into the street. Maybe she could find the boys. They were always somewhere together, and her big brother, Doug, was usually with them. They would ride for hours and hours. When they got tired, they would crash on someone's lawn. Usually, they got Angel to ring the doorbell and ask whoever was home if they could get something to drink from the water hose. Angel didn't mind, as long as she got to hang out with the boys. She was just fine asking anybody anything. She pedaled faster.

As Angel pedaled, she got to thinking about her best friend, Kristine. Kristine was also on Angel's soccer team. Angel didn't think Kristine was very good at soccer. She was pretty, though, much prettier than Angel. She was also smaller and had clothes that always fit her body, which reminded Angel to pull her shirt down to cover her belly while she was riding. She definitely didn't want the boys to see her belly.

Angel kept pedaling looking for her brother's friends.

She wished Kristine wasn't mad at her anymore.

That had not been a good day. Kristine got mad about what happened last week at their coach's house. The whole team was trying on new jerseys. Angel had to get the largest jersey, and it was really big. It was kind of embarrassing, and she got a little teary-eyed, but she tried not to cry in front of all the girls. Angel tried real hard to be tough.

But ever since that day, Kristine had acted funny toward her. It was also the day she accidentally told her mom about the fishing trips. Angel didn't mean to. It just came out of her mouth after she and her mom got into an argument about the jersey. Angel had a hard time keeping her mouth shut. She felt that if she had a mouth, she had a right to use it.

It started after she and her team finished trying on jerseys.

"Angel, can you go get your mom?" asked Angel's coach.

"Sure coach, I'll go find her," Angel said, still wearing her brand-new extra-large youth jersey that barely covered her upper body.

Angel went to find the bathroom before she went to search for her mom. When she turned the corner, she saw her mom and Kristine's mom. They were arguing over something. Angel hid behind the corner so she could hear what they were saying.

Kristine's mom said, "Fammy, you said you would give me that money back, and you also promised that you would pay me for the bike."

"I have it at the house. I just forgot to bring it."

"Really? Because you have been saying that for a while, and I also know you haven't paid for Angel's soccer dues. Or are you going to skip on that too?"

Fammy raised her finger and pointed it at Kristine's mom and started yelling in Dutch. Angel cringed and realized she needed to rescue Kristine's mom because this was gonna get bad.

"Why are you yelling, Mom?" she rounded the corner in

sight of them both and looked at Kristine's mom trying to look sorry for what her mom had said or done.

Fammy turned and saw Angel, "Grab your stuff, *laanjagen!*" Angel knew her mom was mad because she only spoke Dutch when she was super angry. That word meant to hurry up.

Fammy looked at Angel, and continued speaking in loud Dutch phrases, and stormed out of the house. She didn't even wait for Angel.

Angel grabbed her soccer things and quickly told her team and coach goodbye.

"Um, my mom isn't feeling well, I'll get her to call you," Angel told her coach.

Angel looked at Kristine to say she was sorry, but Kristine was standing by her mom, and wouldn't look at Angel. In fact, when Angel looked at her, she saw Kristine purposely hide behind her mom.

Angel ran outside, and saw her mom, smoking her cigarette.

"What's wrong? What happened? Do I have to give my bike back to Kristine?" Angel asked. She knew she shouldn't have said that, but she really really loved the bike.

"All you care about is yourself and that stupid bike and this nonsense soccer crap. You are a selfish little girl," Fammy responded. She walked faster. Angel could barely keep up with her as they walked toward the bus stop. As Fammy walked, her long reddish-brown hair would swing. Even in her anger, she looked like a model.

Angel looked at her mom and could not stop the words that flowed from her mouth, *Don't say it, Angel, don't say it.* But she said it.

"No, I'm not selfish, you are. You are selfish. You always mess things up for me. For Becca and Doug. Always. Just like at Christmas when you sold all of our presents," Angel yelled at her mom.

Fammy was even more irritated. "I told you why we had the yard sale. We were moving, and we couldn't take all those toys you and your brother and sister had. Especially all your sister's crap magazines."

Fammy took a long drag of her cigarette and threw it to the ground. She used her foot to stomp it out. Angel watched her twist her foot to put out the cigarette butt.

"But we didn't move! And it was three days after Christmas that you sold my brand-new Little Professor calculator. That was the only thing I wanted from Santa! I needed that for my math class," Angel said as they continued walking toward the bus stop.

Fammy grabbed Angel's hand hard and said, "There are things you don't understand. I try hard. Mike tries real hard to make sure you kids have everything; he works hard."

Fammy took out another cigarette, and lit it, took a long drag, and looked up to the sky.

Angel looked at her mom and said, "Is that why I have to rub him when we go on fishing trips?"

She realized when she said it, she should not have. She should have just shut up, but it came out before she could stop it.

Fammy turned her head to the side, and with wide eyes said, "What kind of rubs? What are you talking about?"

Angel knew she had said something she wasn't supposed to say. Mike, her stepdad, had told her to keep that between them. He called it their "special moments" on their trips. She just stared at her mom. "Nothing, never mind, let's just get on the bus."

"Angel, what are you talking about? None of that is true.

You don't rub him, you stupid child," Fammy said in disgust again.

Fammy walked faster and Angel walked beside her. They walked until they reached the bus stop and sat down on a graffiti-written bench.

Angel was thankful there were other people there, so they wouldn't have to talk.

Angel hated it when people called her stupid. She wasn't stupid. She was smart, her teacher told her how smart she was, and she always knew the answers to everything.

They sat there in silence until the bus came. They got on the bus and sat near the back.

Angel finally turned to her mom and said, "He asks me to rub between his legs until something comes out. He calls it his magic time, and then I get to stop. Then we get to fish. And you are stupid back!"

"You are a little liar, shut your damn mouth!" Fammy responded and slapped her across the face. Angel looked at her mom and was shocked. For the first time, Angel didn't know what to say. Why did her mom slap her? She was not a liar. She was telling the truth. She looked around; nobody would look at her. Nobody cared.

Nothing had changed in the week since. Angel pedaled and pedaled. She wondered how fast someone could pedal. Could she pedal fast enough to go far away? Maybe she could live on the railroad tracks. Maybe she could pedal fast enough she could go into the future? Maybe then she wouldn't have to rub Mike anymore and he wouldn't rub her. She wouldn't have to sit still as they watched fireworks, as Mike would sneak behind her and put his eyes on her boobies, which she didn't even have. Her sister had some, but Angel didn't. She had fat, tons of fat that poked out.

She saw a picture of an angel one time, and it was fat. So she could be a fat Angel with a belly.

A big belly, which reminded her to pull her shirt down. She pedaled and pedaled.

If Angel had the right clothes that fit her and did not have to wear her mom's tiny clothes, maybe her fat wouldn't hang out. But her mom wouldn't buy her clothes. She just had to wear her Mom's hand me downs, because her mom never bought her and her brother or sister clothes. Angel would go through a big stack of clothes in her mom's bedroom to find something that would fit her body and big belly. They were really weird clothes with flowing sleeves and big bell bottom pants. Angel hated them. She wanted to wear shorts, and t-shirts, and clothes with Shawn Cassidy on them.

So what if her mom didn't believe her? She knew she was not a liar. She didn't make up the story of what Mike did to her. It really happened. She might have a fat belly and ugly clothes, but she wasn't a liar.

Angel had read a book a long time ago about a girl that went down a hole and met some really cool animals, so ever since then, Angel pretended that's where she was when she wasn't happy. Rabbit holes were dark, and in them, everyone there could be who they really were supposed to be. That is where she went when her mom didn't believe her, it was a great place to be sometimes.

But all that happened last week, and as of today, she still had her bike. Now she was going to find her brother and his friends playing stickball, then she would ask them to let her play.

She was better than they were anyway.

Angel could run faster than them, and she was smarter than they were too. She loved staying out all day until the sunset. She didn't have a lot of friends, mostly because they haven't lived in the area that long, and the girls in their neighborhood all wanted to play with dolls and stuff. She wanted to play with her brother. She loved riding with his group. Sometimes they would all ride their bikes through the orange groves and play hide and seek. Angel always got pushed to the back, but she didn't care. She would just keep pedaling on her groovy bike until she found them.

They were somewhere in this neighborhood.

Who knows, maybe if she couldn't find them, she'd just ride her bike all the way downtown and spend the day looking at the graffiti. She loved to look at all the chaos and color that was so bright on the buildings.

Ventura was so big to Angel. It wasn't quite as big as Los Angeles, where they lived before, but it was pretty big.

She also loved to look at the old missions in the downtown part. Sometimes her mom would let her skip school and she and her sister would go into all the old shops. Her mom would disappear for a couple of hours. Those were days that she and her mom got along.

She also couldn't forget about the beach. She loved the beach, she loved to watch the surfers and those big white waves. They didn't get to the beach often, but she loved it when they went.

Yeah, that's what I'll do, Angel thought.

She would ride until she found the beach. She rode faster toward the end of the street, and as she peddled, her wild bushy hair flowed in the wind, her chubby cheeks showing her joy, but in her small innocent mind, she wondered if any of the people that painted graffiti ever went fishing with little girls, lived on the railroad tracks, and had to go down rabbit holes to escape.

CHAPTER 4

HERO

ANGEL WAS SINGING at the top of her lungs her favorite song, "Believe it or Not." It was her theme song, from her favorite tv show *Greatest American Hero*. She loved the lyrics.

She loved the phrase "believe it or not, I'm walking on air, flying away so free," or something like that. If she could fly, then anything would be possible. She could fly away from this parking garage in Van Nuys and see the world.

She could find her real father, and he would protect her. He would buy her clothes like all the cute girls had at school; she wouldn't have to wear the same clothes every day. She could be pretty, popular, and everybody at school would stop making fun of her.

She would tell that boy on the bus to shut up because her dad would get him.

That stupid boy on the school bus. She hated him, he made fun of her and Becca every day. She recalled what he said earlier that day.

Boy: "You know that you are almost the ugliest person in the school."

THE BOOK OF ANGEL

Angel looked away. She tried to ignore him.

Boy: "Hey ugly fat girl, you have got to be the ugliest dumbest girl on the bus, can't you hear me? Or are you deaf too?"

With that, Angel had enough, and she responded back: "If you turned around, you wouldn't have to look at the school's ugliest girl. So shut up and leave me alone!" Angel fought back tears. She would not, she could not let him see her cry.

Boy: "Why do you wear the same clothes every day? Your clothes are so old-looking, and you have no boobs."

Angel: "Shut up, you don't know what you are talking about, shut up!"

The boy turned around, the bus stopped. Angel was relieved when he gathered his backpack to get off the bus. She thought he finally had shut his mouth, but then he turned around one more time and said, "You know why you aren't the ugliest girl in the school? Because your sister is."

Angel jumped up and hit him right in the back as he was walking off the bus. She didn't care if the bus driver saw her or not. She hit him as hard as she could. He flinched, and everyone on the bus laughed.

"You let a girl hit you," yelled someone from the back.

"Yeah, and an ugly one, too!" said someone else.

It took everything Angel had not to turn around and go after the boys in the back, but she couldn't because she and her sister couldn't get kicked off the bus. If they got kicked off, her mom would get mad, so Angel had to keep her mouth shut.

She sat down and crossed her arms over her chest. Face as red as an apple. She closed her eyes and imagined she was a rabbit going into her hole.

But that was earlier today, and right now she was going to spin around and around and sing her favorite song.

Angel just kept singing and twirling around. She kept going until she got so dizzy, she had to sit down.

She flung herself down on the grass and looked up to the sky.

Where was her dad? What did he look like? He would hit that boy so hard he wouldn't know what was coming. One day, when he finally finds her, she would tell him about that boy. He would make it right. She just knew it.

Wonder where he is? She bet that he was in New York City working as a business guy, wearing a business suit and making the big bucks. *I bet that is what he does,* she thought.

She hated boys, most of them were so mean. She didn't know when they decided to become so mean, because she used to hang out with all of them. But in the last year, boys just didn't like her.

She was bigger than most of the boys anyway, but if she was going to be ugly, then so be it.

She also was smarter than most of them. She was always the first one to raise her hand. Well, at least she was better than them at that.

She might not be pretty or popular or wear nice clothes, but she was never mean to people, unless they deserved it. That boy deserved it.

She thought of her favorite lyrics, closed her eyes, and wondered if her dad had been mean when he was her age? He wasn't, she just knew it.

He was probably like this boy named Greg that rides the same bus as her. Greg was pretty nice, sometimes he sat with Angel, but most of the time his mom picked him up from school. He was also in her class at school. Greg was super smart. She liked the school she was at right now, and she was actually in the smart reading group for once. She knew it was the smart group because Greg was in the same group.

She looked at the clouds, and she swore she saw a rabbit. She could make out the face and the ears, and then she saw the tail.

Definitely a rabbit.

She liked rabbits; her reading group was the Rabbit group. The Rabbit group meant that you were a good reader.

She did start in the Turtles reading group when they first moved here because, for some reason, all her school records got lost when they moved. She hated the Turtle reading group. Everyone in that group read so slowly. And they had to pronounce every word slower.

It drove Angel crazy.

It isn't that hard to read, so it got on her nerves so bad when the other students would have to read every single syllable. But Angel never said anything to them, because that would be mean, and she was not going to be mean. Her reading teacher, Miss Rowe, kept telling Angel to stop reading so fast in the group. But eventually Miss Rowe moved her to the Rabbit group.

Angel just laid on the grass and kept looking at the sky, she saw lots of clouds, and they were moving so fast. She couldn't even find her rabbit anymore.

Where did it go? Did it go to God?

Which reminded Angel of a conversation she had with Miss Rowe a couple days ago. Miss Rowe kept Angel inside one day during recess and asked her to read a paragraph from a book.

It was a pretty interesting book to Angel.

"Angel, do you understand that God has given you a gift," Miss Rowe said to her.

Angel looked at Miss Rowe, she never really knew that God gave gifts, especially to her.

She was just learning about this guy named God anyway. She went to church with a couple of people before, when her mom would let her go, so she had heard about this person named God, but didn't know he gave gifts.

"Miss Rowe, I don't really understand what you mean about a gift," Angel looked at Miss Rowe with a puzzled look.

"God gives everyone a gift; some get more than others because God knows what they need. You, my dear, have been given a gift of determination, hope, and resilience. You are called to do something grand. Do you know what that means?" she looked at Angel.

Angel turned her head to the side and stared at Miss Rowe. She always thought Miss Rowe was so neat. She wasn't beautiful, but she had been to so many places that Angel was fascinated by her. Miss Rowe showed slides to the class of her in Peru and riding on a llama. Angel never even knew what a llama was.

Angel shook her head.

"Determination and resilience mean that no matter what, you keep the faith, you keep going. You never give up. Hope is what you see without ever really seeing it, it is like knowing that no matter what life throws at you, you will find a way to overcome it. Those are gifts," Miss Rowe patted Angel's head.

Angel had no clue what she was talking about, but she nodded her head up and down like she knew because she didn't want Miss Rowe to think she was dumb.

"Now run outside and play with the other kids," and then she opened her grade book to write something down.

The rabbit in the sky was definitely gone.

Angel kept looking.

She saw an airplane in the sky.

She closed her eyes and thought about the note Miss Rowe sent to her mom last week. Angel opened it because she thought it was a bad note about Angel talking all the time.

The next day, her mom came to the school, and Miss Rowe and her mom had a conference. Angel had to stay outside the classroom, but she heard what they were saying because she could hear them through the small crack in the door.

"Mrs. Burns, I am Angel's teacher and I think she has the potential to skip a grade, but there are no school records. When our school secretary tried to find them from Angel's last school, they could not locate any. Could you provide me with the correct school so we can get her records," Angel heard Miss Rowe ask her mom.

Angel's mom didn't say a word. Fammy took out her Salem Light and her lighter and lit her cigarette. She took a deep drag and then blew out the smoke while she stared at Miss Rowe

Angel was already embarrassed by the way her mom was dressed. Fammy had a shirt that barely covered her belly, a pair of hip hugger bell-bottom pants, giant gold rings on all her fingers, and makeup that was so thick that Angel could barely see her skin.

"Mrs. Burns, do you understand what I am saying? We need those records. Do you have the records?"

Angel got up and walked into the room because she knew her mom was about to get angry, "Sometimes she has a hard time with English." Angel said to Miss Rowe, interrupting the conversation.

"She wants our school records," Angel said to her mom.

Fammy looked at Miss Rowe and said in broken English, "How dare you say I not a good mother. I a good mother, you don't know anything."

Fammy took another drag of her cigarette and gathered her large, flowered hippie bag.

"I'm not accusing you of anything, I just want Angel to get the best education she can. She is very smart, she can do great things," said Miss Rowe.

Fammy took another drag, "That one? Great things? You don't know anything. She is selfish and will not shut up."

Fammy looked at Angel and yelled in Dutch. "*Angel, laten we gaan, we zijn hier klaar*," which meant, "get your stuff we are done here."

Angel opened her eyes and wiped a tear. She lay on the ground and stared at the sky.

She hated when her mom acted like she didn't understand what she was saying. Her mom always used the excuse that she was from the Netherlands and had a hard time understanding English. But Angel didn't think that was the reason; because every time they moved, their school records would somehow get lost. She asked her mom one time why they couldn't just get a copy of their records and keep them, so when they moved, they would have them. Her mom just looked the other way.

Angel thought it was because her mom always would make them move in the middle of the night, which she thought was an odd time to move, but the landlord couldn't find them at night. She also secretly thought that maybe her mom was keeping her from her dad, and that's why they moved all the time.

She wasn't dumb.

Maybe God would give her a dad, maybe he could be her hero from the song and then should could stay here and stay in the Rabbit reading group. She was happy here, and she could lay on this grass forever and not think of anything but good things.

Maybe she could become friends with popular pretty

skinny girls because they would think how smart she is being part of the Rabbit group. Or they would like her because she had a really smart rich dad.

Today was a good day, and maybe she would be able to get moved into the smart math group, and then perhaps she could start to find some friends. She got up and start spinning again. She sang louder, "Believe it or Not, I'm flying on in, hoping to find my way."

She didn't know if those were the words, but they sounded so good to her.

Angel didn't know how long she was out there, but eventually, she heard a voice.

"Angel, Angel, you need to come inside," yelled her big brother from the top of the garage parking lot.

"No, I'm staying out here, and you're not my dad, so shut up." The last dad Angel had was Mike, and he left the night he came home and found her mom in the bed with another guy. Her brother needed to shut up and let her keep spinning.

"Look, get your butt in the apartment. We're leaving," said her brother.

"Where are we going, are we going to the store, are we going to the movies?" Angel got really excited. She loved going places. She walked toward her brother, still a little dizzy from all that spinning.

"No, seriously. We're leaving and headed to a hotel," her brother told her.

"Mom said we can't stay here anymore. We don't have the money to pay the rent. We have to go," he added.

"No! No! No! We aren't, you're just saying that to be mean to me! I am not going!" She stopped in her tracks, and folded her arms across her chest, and stomped her foot. "I am not going. You can't make me!" Angel yelled.

"I don't have time for this. Stop being a baby. See you at the apartment," said her brother as he turned and walked back.

Angel watched him walk away and shouted, "You are always mean to me. You are playing a joke! Shut up! Where are we going? Do I need my jacket?" Angel just knew that none of it was true. Doug was just playing a trick.

Angel walked up the hill of the garage lot.

It couldn't be true.

Angel got closer to the apartment.

Angel opened the door, and there was her mother.

Her mother had a cigarette in her mouth, and Angel thought she had way too much makeup on again.

She saw her mom hurriedly packing what little belongings they had into brown grocery store bags.

"What's going on? We are not moving!" Angel said to her mom.

Fammy didn't say a word. She just kept putting stuff in grocery bags.

"Why are we going to? Why can't we stay here" I just got moved to the Rabbit group, I'm not going!" Angel said to her mother, her arms folded across her chest in defiance.

Fammy said, "Get your stuff; we can't fit a lot, so just get what you need, actually just get what you can fit in your backpack. *Haast je.*"

Angel looked at her sister Becca, who was sitting in the corner, holding a packed bag on her lap, pretending to read a book, because she knew their lives were about to be turned over again, just like the last time.

Becca was always reading a book or a magazine. She always escaped into her books, just as Angel had escaped into rabbit holes.

Angel wanted to kick the book out of her sister's hands.

Angel looked up and wished this God up there would do something. Why didn't he step in and be a hero? All she could do was think about how she wasn't going to be in the Rabbit group anymore.

Where was her hero? she wondered. *God, she needed a hero right now.* Angel closed her eyes, clenched her fist, and wished as hard as she could for her hero to come find her and take her away. She wished so hard her eyes started to hurt, but all she heard was her mom yelling for her to get her stuff packed into her backpack.

She closed her eyes harder and thought of the boy that called her ugly, she thought of the rabbit group, she thought of the little girl that went down the rabbit hole, she didn't know what gift Miss Rowe said she had but she guessed it really didn't matter now.

She didn't have any superpowers to make her a hero.

All she had was a brown paper bag and a backpack. Her shoulders dropped, her eyes opened, and she packed her bags.

She was going down the rabbit hole.

CHAPTER 5
LONG BEAUTIFUL NAILS

FAMMY USUALLY STAYED gone at night.

Angel had recently found out at school what the words "whore" and "prostitute" meant. She'd said it in class one day when she was describing a character in a book. She'd thought it meant a woman that was able to get a lot of boyfriends and make money like her mom.

Angel's teacher wasn't happy at all with her, and she had to sit at recess. Her teacher definitely wasn't Miss Rowe from her past. Angel learned what the word whore really meant when her mom brought home a man from her night of dancing.

Sometimes Angel would stare at her mom just because of her beauty. She had perfect facial features. Her hair was long, thick, and brownish-red. She often helped her mom dye it when a little bit of gray would start to shine through.

She just wished her mom was as beautiful inside as she was outside.

They didn't have a car and often had to walk to the store to buy groceries if they missed the city bus.

They always had to buy her mom cigarettes and of course

her hair dye before they bought groceries. They never really had enough money to buy all the groceries when they got there, sometimes they would bring all pennies, nothing but pennies. The cashier would get so upset when Angel would pull out the money bag, and she had to count the change. Angel would look away so she didn't have to see the look of disgust on the cashier's face. Sometimes they would have to put things back because the pennies were just not enough. Angel knew they needed bread and milk, but they couldn't afford those, but Fammy always had cigarettes.

Other times Angel would take some change and buy the cigarettes for her mom by herself. She would walk across the busy highways and streets, dodging cars, and riding her new skateboard. Angel would put the money in the vending machine and out popped the cigarette pack.

She always wanted to make sure her mom had the cigarettes, Salem Lights, because things would get worse with her mom if she didn't have them. Her mom would start yelling and shaking if she didn't have them.

Fammy always had one lit up in her hand.

As soon as they would leave the store, Fammy would pull out the cigarettes with her long beautiful nails take a long slow drag, and they would start the walk back home.

If they were lucky, her mom would find a nice man coming out of the store and ask him if he could give them a ride home. Angel's mom would toss her hair back behind her shoulders, bite her bottom lip, and ask the man so sweetly to take them home.

Angel heard her tell a man one time that her husband had died in Vietnam and left them all alone with no money, which was a bald-faced lie.

It was the first time Angel had heard that story.

Surely her dad didn't die, and her mom had kept that from her and her siblings?

Her mom was good at finding people to take them home, and Angel suspected that Fammy just said that so they could get a ride home.

No one could resist Fammy's charm.

Angel sat by the hotel pool. Their new, temporary home.

It was pretty nasty, she thought. Green and black stuff was around the edges, and it smelled awful.

It wasn't like this was a real hotel anyway. People pretty much lived here year-round, at least Angel and her family did. There were a lot of families that lived in this hotel. In some ways it was like an apartment complex, only each apartment had one bedroom.

Angel and her brother and sister pretty much did whatever they wanted to do here. They would roam the streets and hop on the city bus.

Becca mostly stayed in the hotel room and read.

Nights were the worst.

That's when you heard sirens, couples fighting, kids crying.

They would all huddle in the room together alone, most of the time without their mom.

If Fammy was home, Angel, Becca, and Fammy would sleep in the one bed, and her brother on the floor.

Sometimes Fammy would come in at night with a man, then her mom would kick them out of bed, and she and her siblings would all be on the floor to sleep for the night.

Angel tried hard not to laugh or make noise when her mom was in bed with the strange man, but it was hard not to because of all the strange, awful sounds her mom and the strange men would make while in bed.

She and her brother would put their hands over their mouth to keep from making noises.

One time, her mom brought home a man, and he got really mad when he found out that she had kids in the room. He started yelling at her and saying things like she was a bad mom for bringing him into a room with her kids and even called her a whore.

She heard her mom asking the man for money. That was when Angel realized that her mom was a prostitute—a whore. Her mom sold sex for money.

Angel looked at the dirty pool again.

It reminded her of her stepfather Mike but Mike was gone.

After Angel had mentioned the fishing trips, her mom and Mike argued. After a big fight one night, Fammy came into Angel's room and started yelling at her saying she made it up because Angel wanted Mike gone. Angel screamed back that she didn't make it up, but Angel sensed that Fammy still thought she did.

And then one day soon after that, Angel, her brother, and sister came home from school, and all their stuff was gone. There was a truck outside with a man driving it. Fammy hopped in the front seat and told Angel, Becca, and Doug to get in the back of the bed.

They rode down the highway with the wind in their face.

The rest of the way, Angel stayed in her rabbit hole.

That seemed so long ago. When she lived in Ventura, at least her life was a little predictable. She was eleven now, and she believed they'd lived in six different locations since then. She lived in Ventura, Semi Valley, North Hollywood, somewhere in LA, and now she didn't know where she was living.

They'd missed so much school, and when they did go,

she didn't understand half of what her teachers were saying anyway, especially her math class.

The pool was really dirty, thought Angel.

Angel was able to make out some kind of blurry image alongside the lining in the pool.

She had to squint really hard to see what they were. Turtles? Bunnies?

She wondered how long ago those bunnies were shiny and new.

She could barely see the pool, and barely see the board at school.

Her new teachers thought she was dumb, but Angel still kept trying, even though Math was so confusing. She had missed so much school, and she could barely see the board, her glasses had broken awhile back, and for the first time, school was hard. She liked her social studies and science class, though, she loved learning about the past. It never changed, which was ironic to Angel because her life was always changing. Her science class was usually interesting.

She loved learning about animals and the weather. She tried real hard in those classes, but most of the time she was just so tired, hungry, or had a headache so it was hard to focus or stay awake. She never had the right stuff for class anyway. She always had to borrow paper and pencils, and her classmates just rolled their eyes and told her no. Her teachers got mad when she didn't have supplies, so she just sat there and went down rabbit holes. And then she would just put her head down, it didn't matter anyway, she didn't have anything to write with anyway.

Who cared at this point? Angel sure didn't anymore.

Her mom just didn't care if they went to school or not, and honestly, Angel wasn't so sure if school was her thing anymore either. She found herself staying in her rabbit hole more and more these days. Her mom had started talking about a guy she had met, and Angel had noticed that her mom was changing. She was jittery all the time, and didn't seem herself.

"*Angel, kom binnen,*" yelled her mom from inside the hotel room, which meant come inside. Their hotel room was steps away from the pool.

Angel walked into the room and saw a man sitting on the bed with her mom. Angel instantly knew something was not right with this man. She could feel it in her gut.

He must have come in the morning, while Angel, Doug, and Becca were roaming the streets around the hotel with the other hotel kids.

The man had a pair of fingernail clippers and was cutting her mom's long, gorgeous nails. She had always been proud of them and kept them painted and filed.

In the one-bedroom hotel room, there wasn't much room for anyone. Angel stood there as Becca and Doug sat on the bed with her mom and the man.

Angel just couldn't understand why her mom's nails were being cut short.

All three of them watched this stranger clipping their mom's nails short. Angel didn't understand why her mom was letting this man cut her nails short.

"Mom, why are you cutting your nails short? You love your nails long," Angel finally spoke up.

The man sitting next to her mom looked at Angel and smiled.

But it wasn't a good smile.

To Angel, it was a smile that was grimacing, evil, and piercing. Angel automatically did not like him.

She didn't like his hair, which was bleach blonde, and not real, almost like he was wearing a wig.

Angel thought he looked a lot like the actor Burt Reynolds. Almost like he was trying to look like the actor. Living in California, she saw a lot of actors. The other day, she walked around in Toys "R" Us and saw Lee Majors and Farrah Fawcett. She knew who they were because she used to watch Charlie's Angels all the time.

She wanted to be an angel at one time; only she was chubby and not pretty like the angels were on the show.

But she was smart and knew she could solve mysteries. Well, she used to be smart. But most of the time, she knew who committed the crime before the show was even over. It would drive her brother and sister nuts. They would all look at her and say, "Shut up, Angel, we don't care." She would yell it out anyway.

The man was much bigger than her mom, and he just looked mean.

He looked at Angel's mom and said, "I cut them short. I'm sick of her scratching me all the time. She wanted them short, isn't that right, Fammy?"

Fammy answered, "Yes, Angel, I like them short. It will be all right."

Fammy looked at her three children and said, "This is Frank. He is going to be your new dad. I want you guys to call him Dad."

Angel looked at the man sitting on the hotel bed, and her gut told her again that things were not right.

They were far from right. Things were bad.

She looked at her brother and sister, and they had the same look on their face. Angel felt evil, like a bad feeling.

In science, she learned that every animal is born with a

natural way to feel bad, and sometimes it was called a gut feeling. Angel even read the bunnies have the same kind of feeling. Well, she had a very, very bad gut feeling.

"You all go outside and wait by the pool. We'll come get you later," Frank told them.

Fammy nodded her head.

Angel opened the door, and her siblings followed, and Angel sat in the exact spot she was in earlier. She closed her eyes, and went down her rabbit hole. As the day turned into evening, Angel was getting hungry.

"I'm going in the room to find out when dinner will be," Doug stood up and told Angel and Becca.

"Good, because I am starving," Angel said as her stomach growled.

Doug knocked on the door. There was no response. Doug knocked again.

Frank opened the door and pushed Doug so hard he fell on the payment.

"When we are good and ready, we'll let y'all in? You understand?" Frank yelled at Doug. "Now, y'all get your asses in the room."

Angel, Becca, and Doug walked into the room.

Angel had enough of this man taking over their room, cutting her mom's nails, and she was starving. She could no longer tolerate this mean man, she had to say something.

"When are you leaving? We only have one bed in this room, and we all share it. It's late, and we're hungry."

Frank looked at Angel. He got right in her face as if he was about to hit her. Instead, he pushed her on the bed and said, "Shut your damn mouth. If I ever hear your mouth again, I will slap it so fast you won't know what hit you. Your mom has told me about you, and your big mouth. You won't speak like that ever again. You understand?"

Angel looked up at Frank. She looked at her mom. Her mom looked away.

"All of you go outside until we are done. We'll cook something, and then we'll come get you," Fammy told Angel, Becca, and Doug.

They found themselves again sitting by the pool, Angel looked up in the sky that was beginning to turn dark. She wondered where this God was. Where was her dad?

The three of them sat by the pool in silence, and Angel longed for the days of riding bikes, city busses, reading in her Rabbit group, and watching Charlie's Angels. Maybe she would never be pretty or smart enough to ever become a Charlie's Angel and her mom's beautiful nails were no longer beautiful.

She went down her rabbit hole.

CHAPTER 6

LOST IN THE COLD

THEY STOPPED IN front of a church, and Angel was so cold.

Her teeth were chattering.

Her bones hurt from the cold.

It was snowing outside, and they were somewhere in Nevada.

Angel was just so tired of being cold.

She tried to use her jacket to keep her warm. They had stopped at a Salvation Army store a couple of days ago, and they were all able to pick out a free jacket. In California, they never had to wear jackets like this; she hated this jacket. It reminded her of everything that was not right in her life right now. It had fake fur around the collar that looked like a rabbit, and it was yellow. She hated yellow. When she was trying on jackets, they were all too big, and she didn't have many choices. Angel wasn't used to being small, she knew she grew a couple of inches, but Angel had not realized that she had lost weight. But who wouldn't lose weight living in a car and eating from convenience stores?

She couldn't even remember the last time they had eaten.

Frank would stop and get them hot chocolate, but rarely did they ever get food. He said the liquid would keep them feeling full. But Angel was still hungry.

She knew that they had run out of money already because she saw him and her brother running out of the convenience store with hot dogs under their shirts. She saw the 7/11 manager come running out shouting at them. They were running as fast as they could back to the car. Frank was yelling at her mom to start the damn car. Her mom even did a wheelie coming out of the parking lot as she drove the car away.

Angel heard the word damn a lot, and also other cuss words. She wasn't used to that, her mom always cussed in Dutch. Frank cussed all the time.

"Damn, that old guy was blind as a bat," Frank said.

My brother nodded his head in agreement, "Damn, blind guy."

Angel's brother had just started to cuss when he talked, but she thought he was doing that because Frank kept telling him he was a sissy. Angel even saw Frank hit him in the head one time and tell him to toughen up.

Angel didn't want her brother to toughen up, she liked him the way he was. *Frank needed to shut up,* she thought. But she couldn't dare say that, so she told herself to shut up and not to say anything.

She told herself that a lot.

Frank threw the hot dogs in the back seat, "Eat these"

Angel said, "These are cold. I have never had a hot dog that was cold before."

Just as soon as she said it, she regretted it because before she could even bite into the hotdog, Frank slammed on the brakes, put the car in park, and reached across the seat. He grabbed Angel and hit her in the mouth, knocking her hotdog to the old car's floor.

Her mouth was pouring blood from the hit.

"Shut your mouth and eat the damn hotdog. Ungrateful bitch. Eat it, or never eat again," Frank ground out.

Angel didn't mean to say it. She had just told herself not to say anything, her mouth always got her in trouble.

She looked at her mom for help, but instead, Fammy turned her head away from her, looked outside the window of the car.

"I just meant that I hadn't eaten a raw hotdog. I didn't...I didn't know." Angel said under her breath, holding her bleeding mouth.

Doug and Becca, her brother and sister, sat in the back seat and silently ate their raw uncooked hotdogs. They were too scared to say anything.

"You know what? Give your hot dog to them, you don't deserve to eat," Frank said.

"But I'm hungry. I'm sorry. I'm sorry. I'll eat the hot dog," Angel said as she was picking it up from the old car's floorboard.

Blood dripped from her hand to the floorboard.

She tried to shove the hotdog in her mouth, but Frank jerked the hotdog out of her hand.

"No, little bitch. You'll learn to stop running your big mouth and be grateful. Give your hotdog to your sister. While you hand it to her, tell her how much you would like to eat the hotdog, but you can't because you are a little ungrateful bitch. Do it!"

Angel looked at the dirty hotdog and didn't want to say anything to her sister. She just wanted to run away. She looked down at the floor of the old car.

She wanted to go to her rabbit hole.

Frank glared at her and brought his hand to motion that he was going to hit her again.

Angel flinched, and tucked her head into her chest, reached out her hand with the hotdog in it, looked at her sister while sobbing, and said. "Here is my hotdog, I would like to eat it, but I am not thankful."

Angel felt the hit to her head again. "I said for you to say 'ungrateful bitch.' Say it! You will learn your lesson, little bitch."

Angel said, "I am an ungrateful bitch," and quickly looked down.

She was so hungry, her stomach growled loudly, and now her head and mouth hurt.

Her whole body was trembling with fear.

She was trying so hard to block everything out, and just go into her rabbit hole.

Frank said, "That's what you get. Do it again and see what happens."

Angel turned away from her siblings as Frank put the car in drive.

She had tears pouring from her face, but not because she was hit or hungry. Angel was frightened and felt like a wounded rabbit.

She didn't understand why her mom didn't even say anything. Why would she just turn her head?

She felt her brother reach over and hold her hand so that Frank couldn't see his hand over hers. She felt her sister grab her other hand and squeeze it. Although Angel had their hands in hers, she'd never felt so alone in her life. She closed her eyes and retreated into her rabbit hole, where she stayed longer than ever before.

As days turned into weeks, Angel figured out they were traveling across the states. She was so tired of sleeping and sitting in the car's tiny seat, but most of all she was just so frightened.

She heard Frank say they were on their way to Georgia, where Frank, her new "Dad," was from.

She was beyond hungry. And she didn't want Frank as her dad.

They had been living in this car since they left the hotel so long ago.

Her brother and sister had learned quickly not to make Frank mad.

The tiny back seat was so miserable, she had to sit on the hump. Her backside was killing her, but she didn't dare say anything.

It wasn't made for three people in the backseat, but because she was the smallest, she had to sit on the hump.

The old Angel would have said something to Frank about how it isn't fair that she had to sit on the hump the whole time.

But she had changed so much in such a short time.

Angel didn't know if it was because of the car, this ride, or this man.

All she knew was that her life sucked right now, she was just so cold, hungry, and frightened.

She watched the scenes go by on the highway as they traveled.

She saw cars full of kids with families.

She saw moms singing with their kids.

One time she saw a family on the side of the road. It looked like they had a flat tire. When they drove by, Angel thought the dad would be yelling or something, but he didn't look too mad. She wondered what their last names were. Probably some last name like Jones or Smith. Angel wondered if they were happy and if the man loved the mom. She wondered if that was their real dad.

They looked happy, but what did Angel know about happiness anymore? She was trying so hard to keep hoping that things would get better, she just had to. Miss Rowe had told her that she had that gift, but Angel couldn't find it.

And her hope was slowly fading.

Most of the time, Angel just stayed in her rabbit hole, where she was safe and couldn't feel anything. It was dark. Cold, but safe.

At some point during the trip, Angel had figured out that the car they were riding in was stolen. She also figured out that Frank was a real-life bad guy, like wanted by the police for crimes that he had done. Angel heard him talk about robbing people, selling drugs, and stealing cars.

She had overheard Frank talking to her mom about staying away from the police because he "borrowed the car from a friend." Angel would have asked them why they needed to do that, but she learned not to say anything, and she was still smart enough to figure out why they had to stay away from the police. At least Frank hadn't taken away her ability to reason.

She figured the less she said was easier because then she wouldn't have to get hit or watch her brother or mom get hit.

Getting hit in the head or punched in the side was a pretty regular thing now.

She'd witnessed Frank hit her mom so hard, that some of her teeth had come out.

All of them had learned not to say anything.

Angel also learned to agree with everything Frank said, even if she knew he was wrong.

They had long run out of food, and now they had begun to dodge police cars pretty regularly.

It was almost like a game, and sometimes Angel would wonder if, in fact, they were all now criminals. Maybe she was a criminal, and this was her life now. Who would have thought she, fat, (well not now) brown-headed, blue-eyed was now a real-life Bonnie? Bonnie was the only woman criminal she knew, and it was from watching a movie one night with her brother called *Bonnie and Clyde*.

There were times when he and Fammy would sleep for hours and not even wake up. They mostly did it after smelling some weird stuff or smoking their small cigarettes, and sometimes they would take these little, tiny pills. Other times they would put some white powder on the dash and snort it through a straw.

Frank would pull over at a rest stop and he and Fammy would just fall asleep.

Angel, Becca, and Doug would get out and just sit at the tables.

Her brother and sister would make up games for all of them to play.

To Angel, the minutes were like days. She lost count of how many days they had been traveling. All she knew was that it was cold, and it was the month of December, and they were somewhere still in Nevada stopped at another rest stop. They never really got anywhere even though they were headed to Georgia. Frank would stop and meet people, and Angel thought it was to sell drugs. Sometimes they would stop at empty parking lots, and sometimes they would stay in hotel parking lots. They would take back roads so that the police would not find them.

She saw a sign earlier that day that said, "Reno, Nevada."

She had never been to Reno, but she was amazed when they drove through the city and saw big signs of casinos. She knew there was a movie about casinos and bad people that were part of the mob. She and her brother were sitting at the rest stop picnic table as Fammy and Frank slept in the car. Becca was reading a magazine she'd found in the trash can.

"Doug, I gotta ask you a question," Angel asked her brother.

"What?" Doug said as he was fidgeting with a stick on the table.

Angel could see Frank and Fammy in the front seat of the car as she sat at the table. Frank had his head tilted back, with his mouth wide open and Fammy was asleep on the passenger side. She had her head rested on the window.

Angel asked "What movie is about Reno? You know the movie about the bad people that shoot everyone if you don't pay them money. It's a movie that only older people can see. What's the name of it?

Doug, who probably thought that Angel was going to ask about their current situation, was thrown for a moment on how to answer, answered with a strange accent, "Great men are not born great, they grow great."

"What? Why are you talking in that voice?" Angel punched him playfully in the shoulder. "Shut up, what is it?

Doug said, "That is my impression of a mobster. Pretty good, isn't it?"

Angel just looked at him with a wrinkled face and nodded no, and then and waited for him to tell her the name of the movie.

Doug said, in his best impression of Peter from the television show *The Brady Bunch*, "It's Applesauce and Pork Chops, Sweetie."

"You are a dork, that line is from the *Brady Bunch*. Tell me what movie and what does that mean?" Angel yelled.

Doug put his finger to his lips and whispered. "*Sshhh,* he'll be able to hear you. You have a big mouth, keep it down, and I'll tell you."

Angel lowered her head and glanced at Frank in the driver's seat. He had fallen asleep holding a cigarette or something that looked like it, it was much smaller, and she thought it smelled horrible. He had white drool all over his mouth.

"Okay, so what is the name?" Angel lowered her head and whispered, slow and soft.

"It's the *Godfather,* and ain't about Reno, and it's about Las Vegas and the mob. But I haven't seen it. Yet. I will one day," Doug said to Angel.

"Bet I'll see it first," Angel said to Doug.

Doug responded by hitting her back, and it was much harder than she hit him. "Yeah, sure you will," Doug said to her and put his arm around her shoulder.

Angel rolled her eyes and thought to herself. *He thinks just because he is older he can do things first.*

She was the youngest in the family, she was ten years old. Doug was thirteen, and Becca was eleven. Doug always reminded her of that, even as they traveled in this tiny, smelly old car. One day, she thought she was going to prove him and her sister wrong. She was old enough to memorize lines from movies, and she could see any movie she wanted to.

Doug turned and looked at Angel, "Listen as soon as we can, I promise we will get out of this. I just need to get mom to the side and talk with her. I don't know why she's doing this. It has got to be the drugs."

Angel looked at her brother; he was just as scared as she was. She nodded her head and hoped he was right. She wanted to answer with some smart comment, but she was just too tired, hungry, and cold to come up with one. She was also thankful that for just a small moment, she and her brother could have a conversation that was normal and she wasn't scared of saying anything and being hit.

They stayed at the rest stop all night and part of the next day.

Angel overheard Frank tell her mom that they didn't have any gas.

Angel knew what that meant, they had to find a way to get some money.

They loaded up in the tiny car and drove into a town.

Angel's stomach grumbled with hunger.

She tried to tell herself to find her rabbit hole, but her belly wouldn't let her. She was hungry and her rabbit hole didn't have any food.

Her train of thought stopped when she realized that they had parked in front of a church. Angel knew what her mom and Frank were doing. They would make some sad sob story and go into the church to ask for money. It was a game that they played to get money from churches.

Angel had grown accustomed to being part of that scheme. Her mom would go in with one of the kids, usually her, find the pastor and tell them a story about how the car had broken down, and they spent all their money on getting it fixed. Then the pastor would give them money, bags of food, and they would go on to the next town. Most of the time, she and her brother and sister didn't even get the food or the stuff, because Frank would go and sell it. She never realized what he did with the money, but Angel thinks maybe he bought drugs with it. Or whatever he and Fammy used to make them pass out.

THE BOOK OF ANGEL

Fammy and Frank parked the car, and went into the unsuspecting church, and left them in the car.

Angel, Doug, and Becca passed the time by telling jokes and playing a game called, I Spy.

"I spy with my little eye, something yellow," said Becca.

"It's the sun, idiot," said Doug to Becca.

"No, it's not. It's the yellow curtains in the church window. Duh, Doug. You think you know everything," Becca responded.

"I spy with my little eye black and white and blue," Angel said very loudly.

Doug said, "What could that be? The black cat in the yard?"

"NOPE!" said Angel, this time a little louder.

"Why are you shouting? Chill out!" responded Doug.

"I spy with my eye black, blue, and white!" said Angel as she pointed to the police cars parked behind the car.

All three of them turned and looked behind the car. There were police cars everywhere. At least five of them with police officers standing by the cars. Angel even thought they had guns drawn, she wasn't sure though.

"There are blue lights behind us, oh my God. They have got us. They have got us good!" Angel said.

Angel, Doug, and Becca's eyes were as big as the lights shining through the back window.

They heard a voice from a loud megaphone.

"Get out with hands high, one at a time," said a police officer from outside the vehicle.

Angel's mouth dropped to her chest, "You guys, what do we do? Mom and Frank are inside the church, and we are gonna get shot. Just like Bonnie and Clyde!"

Now while some people under pressure get nervous and start crying, Angel didn't. Angel thought the whole scenario quite funny. All she could think of was trying to get out of this tiny car with her hands up, with this God-awful yellow jacket with fur. She thought this would be a great episode on the television show *CHIPS*.

She was not going to go down any rabbit holes right now.

"What do we do?" Angel looked at her brother for the answer.

Becca started to cry uncontrollably. Angel and Doug, although quite scared, just looked at each other.

"This is serious. We're going to have a record. We're in a stolen car," Becca was screaming at Angel and Doug. Angel didn't think they would get arrested, after all they were just kids.

"Becca, stop. Stop being so overdramatic! They are not after us," Doug put his hand on Becca's shoulder reassuringly.

Angel looked outside the window at all the cop cars. She had never seen so many in her life. There were lights everywhere.

"Should we go outside with our hands up? What should we do?" Angel asked her older brother.

As all three of them were trying to figure out what to do, she saw her mom and Frank walking out of the church with the pastor. The policeman quickly handcuffed them. After about ten minutes, finally, three police officers came to the car.

"Are you kids okay?" asked a police officer.

"Can you tell me why you guys were in a stolen car?" said another one.

Angel and Doug looked at each other and shrugged. She looked at Becca, and she was crying hysterically. Angel didn't know if she should tell the police officer everything. She looked at her brother and waited until he spoke. Angel thought she heard his stomach growl.

Maybe this was finally God's way of sending her a hero? She felt safe, a little, anyway.

"Let's get you kids out of this car so that we can talk. Is that okay with you guys?"

As they climbed out of the car, Angel looked to try and find her mom. Where was her mom? She scanned, and then she saw her; she was down on the ground with her hands behind her back.

Angel screamed, "That's my mom! That's my mom!" and Angel fell in the officer's arms as he led her away from her mom.

Angel went into her rabbit hole as she was being placed into the police car. Her eyes were frozen on Fammy.

CHAPTER 7

HEAT OF THE MOMENT

THE MUSIC WAS blaring so loud. Angel couldn't even hear her thoughts. It was the song by Asia, "Heat of the Moment." She tried to make herself go down her rabbit hole, but the music and pounding in her head were so loud she couldn't even do that.

When Frank and Fammy had gotten arrested a couple of months ago, Angel thought that was their ticket out of this mess.

Angel, Becca, and Doug had been placed into a halfway house. It was a home where preteens and teenagers went for temporary placement until they could figure out what to do with them.

Angel really liked the house. She got to go to church, and she learned so much about the God thing that Miss Rowe was trying to teach her about. They all had school together at the house. A teacher came in and they worked in workbooks on their level. Angel, Becca, and Doug all had the same workbooks.

She even got her own Bible. She didn't really understand

it much, but her favorite verse became a verse about faith. It said faith was the substance that things were hoped for. Angel had to look up the word substance, but she kind of thought it meant that her life was the substance. Like her life was gonna be okay, even though she couldn't see things right now. Like her life was like one of the books in the Bible that she was reading about. Well, that's what she thought it meant, maybe.

But then things didn't stay good, because Frank got released—the guy who stole the car wouldn't press charges—and Fammy went right back to him.

Fammy picked them up one day from the halfway house and then things just got worse.

Fammy and Frank had got enough money to put all of them on a Greyhound Bus, *probably from another church,* Angel thought.

And now, Frank made sure they all suffered.

They were somewhere called Brunswick, Georgia, now.

Angel thought Georgia was so different than California. The weather was definitely different. It was so sticky. Angel would go outside sometimes and have sweat everywhere. The sand gnats were awful too. They were like little bitty mosquitos that would bite the crap out of her arms and legs and fly around her face. She would swing her arms around and around to get them to go away but they wouldn't. She missed seeing the orange groves and the lemon trees of California but seeing peach trees everywhere with their white blooms filled that void. Their little white flowers made her think of little baby bunnies. Winter was transitioning to spring but Angel still felt the cold and dark and the loneliness from it.

Frank had family in Brunswick, and that's why they were here. They were also bad like Frank. Angel didn't like any of them either. They were nothing like the pretty flowers of the peach trees, they were ugly, mean, smelled like skunks and wore dirty clothes.

Angel lay there naked on an old, black leather couch that served as her bed. The leather had holes that dug into her back and made red scratch marks. The couch had holes where the leather had long started to peel and make cracks that were sharp and painful on her body.

She looked over and saw her brother lying naked on his "bed," which was a pile of old clothes.

At the other end of the room was her sister, who was sleeping on an old nasty mattress. The mattress springs had found a way to dig through the mattress and Becca's naked body lay on top of the exposed metal.

Frank would not let them get dressed to go to bed; he told them their punishment was to sleep naked. Angel knew the real reason was that it was much easier for him to get them out of bed already ready for him.

She heard her mother screaming and arguing with Frank in the other room. *God, why won't she just shut up and stop arguing with him? She just keeps making it worse. She goes on and on.* Angel wished she could go to her and tell her to stop. But she couldn't because she knew that if she did, things would be worse for them. All she could do was lay there and act like she was asleep. She tried so hard to go down the rabbit hole. If Frank saw her eyes open, he would jerk her up and hit her over and over again and make her start touching him again. She tasted bile in the back of her throat. *Go down the hole,* she told herself.

"Angel, are you awake," Doug whispered.

"Yes," Angel said.

"Are you okay? Have you stopped bleeding?"

Angel looked down at her hands and saw the blood she had

wiped from her head earlier. She touched her head, and it hurt so bad, but it wasn't bleeding anymore. Angel had a stuffed animal that she was holding, an old dirty bunny. She held on to it tight because it made the pain seem a little less. It was the only personal possession that Frank let her have. It was from a trip to the Salvation Army when they got to Georgia, where they went in search of clothes.

"It's okay. I'm okay," she said, "How about you?"

Doug had just gotten out of the hospital. Doug tried to kill himself last week. He overdosed with some pills he found in the house. Angel and her sister were at school when it happened.

Doug wasn't allowed to go to school because he had to help Frank with his drug business. Angel found out from overhearing Frank and her mom talking that Doug had stolen some pills at the drug house and took the entire bottle. On the way home from the drug run, Frank and Fammy stopped at the 7-11 for some cigarettes, and Doug stayed in the car. When Frank and Tammy were in the store, Doug got out of the car and collapsed in the parking lot. Someone in the store saw him and called for help.

Doug looked awful, his eyes were black and blue because when he got out of the hospital Frank beat him up. Frank made Angel and Becca watch and told them they were not allowed to ever talk to Doug or anyone else about it, or they would all get the same.

"Yeah, I'm okay. Try to get some sleep, okay?" Doug whispered to Angel softly.

Angel closed her eyes and tried to sleep.

Sleep, sleep, but she couldn't. She kept thinking about earlier in the day.

When Angel and Becca got home from school earlier that

day, Frank was not happy, neither was her mom. The stereo had not stopped blaring. She could even hear it from the seat of the school bus when it dropped her off.

Angel finally dozed off, but she was awakened by something above her head, it was Frank. He was above her head. She smelled him, he smelled of marijuana and whiskey. Old whiskey.

Angel felt Frank grab her by the hair and drag her into the living room. Then he went and got Becca and Doug. All three of them sat on the floor, naked, while Frank turned up the music louder and louder. Frank put something under her nose. She shrugged her head away, but he grabbed her neck and made her sniff something under her nose. She thought it smelled horrific. He made his way to Doug and Becca. Angel began to feel very light, like she was floating. She could see and hear but she couldn't react. She saw Frank touch her sister and take her into the bedroom. Angel tried to move but she couldn't. It was like something was making her sit. She felt him lift her and then lay her down. She knew he was touching her—he was on top of her—but she couldn't feel. She knew he was breathing in her ear, but she couldn't hear. Angel just focused on the floating objects in the air. She knew she was going down her rabbit hole, but this time she was in both places. She was in the room with him, but she was also in her hole. She saw Frank's face everywhere, even in her hole. She heard her sister scream, she heard her brother yell, but she couldn't move or speak. She just stared at the floating objects, but at the same time, she was trying to run down her hole. Her feet wouldn't move.

Then in the corner of her eye, she saw her mother come running out of the bedroom with an object.

It was an axe. A huge axe used to chop wood.

Fammy swung the axe, but she missed Frank because it was so heavy.

She swung it again, this time it hit Frank.

Angel saw Frank fall and then get back up. Angel was trying hard to get up, but she couldn't. She was paralyzed by some strange force that made her lay still. Her head was pounding, the room was spinning, and she kept seeing the axe swinging. She was back in the rabbit hole. She saw Frank with the axe.

Frank swung and hit her mother. The axe came down on her mother's neck. Angel closed her eyes. She went further down the rabbit hole, she kept going until it was so dark she couldn't see.

She stayed there.

She wasn't coming out.

CHAPTER 8

ESCAPE

SOMEHOW, THEY ALL survived the last few months.

They now lived in a two-bedroom run-down trailer in a trailer park.

Angel never slept, she never ate, they barely went to school. She just endured, and she stayed in her rabbit hole.

Angel had watched as Fammy hit Frank with an axe, she had watched Frank take the axe and hit her mom in the upper shoulder. They both survived, but neither went and got stitches. Every day she saw the blood run down both of their backs, and they would put washcloths on to stop the bleeding. Angel had to clean up the blood on the floor. The landlord finally kicked them out of the old house probably because they didn't pay rent, and they moved.

The blood was still on the floor when they moved.

Angel and her sister were shadows of who they used to be. Angel would sometimes look in the old, shattered mirror, and see someone staring at her. But she didn't recognize her. She just tried to stay in her hole.

Angel and Becca were a sight to see. Angel had seen pictures of children in concentration camps and they looked like that—super skinny and with extremely uneven short hair. Frank had cut their hair short and because they had gotten lice. They had only got lice because he had let his drug buddies spend the night in the old trailer. He cut it so uneven that neither one of them could even put it in a ponytail. Angel had quit fighting back. They weren't allowed to speak in the house, and if they did get something to eat, it was only because a church down the road had seen Angel, Becca, and Doug outside one day walking around and brought food.

When Frank wanted time alone with Fammy, he would kick them out of the house but they had to stay by the window so he could see them at all times. Sometimes local church members would come by with food and try to visit and invite all of them to church. But Frank told all of them to not say a word, or they would regret it. Angel kept her mouth shut.

Angel tried to talk with her mom about them leaving, whenever Frank left on a drug run, but her mom wouldn't even talk about it; it was like her mom was addicted to Frank.

Angel, Becca, and Doug wanted to go to school every day, it was their only escape. But they were only allowed to go when Frank wanted them gone.

Angel tried real hard to pay attention in class, but she fell asleep almost every day. She wanted badly to listen to her teachers, learn and be part of her classroom. But she couldn't. She didn't have the strength. Every night she lay awake with a knife under her pillow. She made a promise to herself, that Frank would never touch her again. She would either kill him or herself. That was her game plan. She could take the knife and plunge it deep into her stomach. She only hoped that the knife would go far enough fast so that Frank couldn't stop her death. She didn't want her brother and sister to be punished by Frank if she didn't succeed.

That was her plan, and she didn't dare share it with anyone. She stole the knife from the kitchen one night when Frank and Fammy were passed out from an all-night drug binge.

She had a good plan, and she would definitely follow through with it before she went through that again. She could stay in her rabbit hole until that moment happened.

She and Becca attended the same middle school, and Becca was pretty much failing every class. Becca had also stopped trying anymore.

Angel was hanging on with the skin of her teeth, but she couldn't see the board anymore. She needed a new set of glasses. She tried to talk with one of her teachers one time about what was going on at home, but the teacher just shrugged her off. She said that Angel needed to realize that everyone has stuff to deal with, and she would figure it out. Angel knew that Miss Rowe would have never said that to her.

Angel decided that she would just have to figure out how to get her family out of this mess. She talked to God sometimes, she just couldn't figure out why he would allow her and her sister to go through what they were going through. He was supposed to be there all the time, right? So where was he? He wasn't anywhere near her. Her knife was the only option she had right now.

One day, Angel and Becca were walking home from the bus stop, and Angel felt like her gut was talking to her again. It was like she knew something really bad was about to happen. Something was stirring in her gut, like something was speaking to her. She heard it loud and clear.

Leave, is what she heard.

Run. She heard it again

Tonight. She heard it again.

As they rounded the corner, she saw Frank and a bunch of men standing in front of the old trailer that they were renting. Angel felt a cold shudder go through her spine.

Becca and Angel walked up the short steps to get into the trailer and had to walk through the men to get through the front door. Just as Angel thought they had made it safely in the house, Frank grabbed Angel by the hair.

"When I get back, you, me, and Becca are going to have a little chat. You hear me, you little bitch? I know what you are thinking, you are always planning, conniving. Don't think I don't see it. You ain't special. You are white stanky trash, and I'm going to make sure you feel that. You will stop holding that head up so high. I'll break you tonight. You hear me?" Frank said as his eyes pierced into Angel's.

Leave, tonight, She heard it again

Be silent. She heard it again

Angel looked into Frank's eyes and with all her strength she said, "Yes."

"Yes, what? I'm your Daddy, say it! Damn it!" Frank held her head and pulled her hair harder.

"Yes, Daddy," Angel answered.

Frank released Angel, and Angel could hear the chuckles from the men in the front yard.

"She is a feisty little thing, isn't she?" asked one of the men.

Frank laughed, and Angel's spine felt it.

She heard the voice again.

Leave. I will never forsake you, I never left you.

The voice, she heard it speaking to her. She couldn't not listen to it, that's how loud it was in her head.

Angel and Becca walked into the old, tiny, dirty single-wide trailer.

Angel closed the door and closed her eyes.

Is that you God? Are you speaking to me? Are you finally here? Angel asked herself.

Angel sat down and waited. She would not say anything to Becca until she was certain. They had to leave that night; their lives depended on it.

She and Becca sat down in the tiny bedroom, that they shared with Doug. Becca opened a book she got from the school library. Angel just stared and listened to wait until she heard the men leave.

How long would it take? How long would they wait? Would they get a chance to go?

She felt like she waited an eternity. Don't go down her rabbit hole.

Listen, Angel, she told herself.

Eventually, Angel heard the last car leave, and she peeked out the window. She didn't see anyone and knew that this was the time.

This was the last time she would ever let him talk to her or her sister again.

It was the last time he would touch her or her sister.

Okay, God. I'm listening, I'm gonna do it.

Angel took a deep breath.

She didn't know how or what, but maybe this was the moment Miss Rowe had talked about so long ago. She said Angel had a gift. What was it she said? Determination? Being resilient? Hope?

She had to become that person.

She would do this; she would find a way. It was leave or she would be forced to use her other option, which was hiding under her pillow on the makeshift bed in the nasty trailer, and a repeat of what her brother did.

Die or leave. She made her choice.

There is nothing stopping you, you can do the impossible. I can make the mountains move.

She heard the voice again.

It had to be God or she was going crazy.

There wasn't gonna be an option to go down her rabbit hole that evening.

She knew in her heart that if she and Becca did not escape today, they wouldn't make it through the night. She didn't know how she knew, but she knew.

"Becca, let's go. Get your things, we are going," Angel grabbed Becca.

"What do you mean?" Becca looked at Angel with a bewildered look on her face.

"We have to leave. We have to run away. Something bad is about to happen, I know it, and we have to go. We only have a few minutes," Angel grabbed Becca's hand and her book.

"But where will we go, we don't have anywhere to go?" Becca

"I don't know where we are going, but it's gonna be okay. I know in my heart, it will be okay," she looked at her sister, Becca.

She had to convince Becca to believe what she was saying.

"We have got to go. NOW," she looked at Becca, grabbed her by the shoulders, and looked her dead in the eye.

Becca looked at her, and she nodded.

Angel wondered if Becca heard the voice too.

It was getting cold outside, and Angel knew that they would need hats and coats. It was springtime, but the night air was still cold. She didn't know how long they would be on the streets, and they had better be prepared just in case. Angel quickly looked around for something, but all she could find was a baseball hat and brown coat. They both smelled like moldy, old clothes. Angel was sure the jacket and hat were probably already in the trailer before they moved in it. She threw the hat on Becca's head, grabbed the jacket, and they headed out the door.

As they moved through the door, Angel noticed a Bible underneath the table. Frank had let them attend church with his sister about a month ago, and she gave one to them.

Angel grabbed it. Maybe the voice in her head would tell her what to do next or maybe she'd find it in this Bible.

Together they ran out of the trailer door, as fast as they could they ran down the rickety old porch, stepped over bags of trash, and ran towards the back of the property into the woods behind the trailer park.

Angel and Becca ran until they were deep in the woods until they felt safe enough to stop and rest.

They found a road that led to a neighborhood, and they were careful to stay away from the streetlights and any car that went by them. Angel didn't want Frank to catch them.

Angel didn't know how long they walked, but it felt like all night. It was dark, and they would take turns on who would wear the jacket and the hat. They stopped at a park to take a rest and found some food in a dumpster. They found an old baby blanket near the dumpster.

It had some baby bunnies on it, but they were able to make a scarf out of it and wrap it around their necks.

Isn't that ironic? Angel thought to herself.

Bunnies on an old baby blanket wrapped around her neck. It was cold, they were hungry and had nowhere to go, but Angel and Becca laughed like they hadn't laughed in years. They talked about the days of living in California, Barbies, *Grease,* and *Tiger Beat.*

Angel would have loved to go back to those days. They seemed forever ago. Every time they would get sad or scared, they would sing a song from *Grease* or their old favorite shows. They walked and walked and walked.

There was a moment when a homeless person got behind them, or they thought he was a homeless person. He wore a long coat that almost looked like a robe. Angel thought it was kind of weird because he never said anything, just followed them. It was almost like he was watching over them or something. They never felt scared with him behind them. He stayed some distance from them, and when they would turn around, he would wave. But it wasn't like a "Hey, how are you?" wave. It was like a "Hey, I am here if you need me" wave. Angel couldn't exactly describe it, but they felt safe with him behind them. She didn't know how long he was back there, but one moment he was there, and then the next he wasn't.

They tried really hard to stay away from the main road, just in case Frank came looking for them. They had no clue where they were. They had only lived in Brunswick for a little while, and they never went anywhere but to school and the church with Frank's sister.

"I'm so tired and so hungry," said Angel to Becca after a few hours of walking.

"Yeah, me too. Do you think we should try and find something to eat," Becca suggested.

"I don't know what to do, I wish we did. I just don't anymore," Angel said.

Angel felt the tired in her bones. Her body was tired and her mind was tired of trying to figure things out.

Becca looked at Angel, and Angel knew that Becca knew she felt defeated. Angel was trying to act like she had all the answers. Even though Becca was older, Becca wasn't a problem solver like Angel. Becca's gift was always to make peace with people, not to fight back.

Angel had always wished she was more like Becca.

Becca reached over and held Angel's hand, and said, "Why don't we go into that Shoney's restaurant up there on the road and call someone…like the police. We can tell them what has been going on, and maybe we can get the police to finally convince Mom to finally leave him."

Angel didn't even know that there was a restaurant, she had been so focused on figuring out what to do next, she wasn't paying attention. Actually, Becca's plan was the best idea they'd had. She looked at her and nodded her head.

They walked hand in hand into the restaurant.

As Angel and Becca got closer, they both felt that their bravest moment was yet to come. They walked into the door and looked around for a bathroom and a phone.

As they were scanning the restaurant, a woman turned the corner. Angel had to do a double take. There, standing with a tray of water glasses wearing her hair in a bun, was Fammy. They had no idea that their mom was even working at a Shoney's restaurant.

Angel felt that maybe the same voice that told them to leave was the same voice that led them here.

Angel took a deep breath and wondered if they would be safe.

Would their mom tell Frank?

Would she take their side, finally?

She held her breath and could feel Becca do the same.

Fammy looked up from her tray and saw the girls.

To Angel, it was like time stopped.

Don't go down the rabbit hole, Angel told herself.

THE BOOK OF ANGEL

Fammy put the dinner plate on the table and ran toward the girls. She grabbed the girls and wrapped them in her arms. *"Mijn meisjes, mijn meisjes,"* Fammy said as she held the girls.

Angel wanted so badly to feel the warmth from her mother, but it was hard to know if it was real or was this just a show for Fammy's coworkers and manager. Fammy knew what was going on, she heard the girls screams at night, she seen the marks and bruises all over them. Would she choose her girls over Frank?

But maybe they were safe, Angel wanted to believe it. She wanted to believe they were safe, *It's going to be okay.* She took a deep breath, closed her eyes.

Angel and Becca were brought into the back of the restaurant, where the manager placed them until the police could come.

After about an hour, the office was covered with police officers. Becca and Angel told the police everything that had been happening—the abuse, the drugs, everything.

Fammy was standing in the background as the girls were telling their stories.

Angel watched her the whole time she was talking to the police officers.

She saw her mom smoke cigarette after cigarette. Fammy looked so different to Angel in that moment. She didn't look pretty, she looked helpless, frail, and confused. The officers kept asking Fammy questions, and she would just shrug and respond in Dutch. Angel wanted her mom to tell the officers everything and maybe finally be on their side; to put and end to this part of their lives.

After what seemed like hours of Angel and Becca telling what happened, she finally got to tell the police officers about Doug.

"You have got to get my brother. He's with him. He is gonna kill him. I know it. He was going to kill us, but we ran away. He has been messing with us. He hit my mom with an axe. Don't make us go back there."

"Hold on. Hold on, honey. We got you. He isn't going to hurt you anymore. He's wanted by the police for many things, and he will never hurt you again. I promise. We will get your brother. You guys will be together, I promise," the police officer said to Angel.

There were so many police officers covering the back of the restaurant that Angel almost felt like she and Becca were famous. She kept hearing the officers talk about Frank and everything he was wanted for by the police.

The officers didn't know that Angel had overheard them talking while she was drinking her milkshake that the manager gave her.

"Those girls are a walking miracle for getting away. This guy is wanted for murder, rape, armed robbery, kidnapping, and several drug charges. They're lucky to be alive. What was their mom thinking getting mixed up with him?"

Angel shivered. She hoped they were safe.

She walked right up to a group of police officers and tapped one of them on his back and said. "Are you guys going to make sure that we will never have to go back to him?"

"Uh, you weren't supposed to be listening to that. You go on back into the room," the officer responded.

"No, I'm not going back into the room unless you promise me that we are safe," Angel crossed her arms around her little frail body and stood firm.

She didn't need anyone or any voice to tell her that her mind was made up.

The officers looked at her, and then looked at each other. The officer on the right of Angel knelt down, put his hands on Angel's shoulders, looked her in the eye, and said, "I promise you will never ever have to worry about that man ever again."

Angel looked at the officer and she wanted to believe him. She really did, but her gut just didn't speak to her like it had earlier. She had to rely on her own voice right now.

As the night wore on, the officers spoke to her mom about how to get her brother away from Frank and devised a plan.

It was decided that Angel and Becca were placed into protective custody for the night.

"Becca and Angel, you guys are going with Ms. Mary. She is going to get you guys some warm clothes, a warm shower, and a warm bed. How does that sound?"

Ms. Mary looked at Angel. She was wearing a light green top and a pair of black pants. She had shoulder length hair and had the darkest brown eyes Angel had ever seen. She looked straight at Angel.

"Hello girls, I am from the Department of Family and Children Services, my name is Ms. Mary. You guys are going to come with me for a little bit. I have something for you guys. It is called a stress bunny. I have one for each of you. You can squeeze it and it will help you." She handed them both a small, plastic, ugly bunny.

Angel didn't want the stupid bunny. She wanted to be a normal girl that has normal things happen like sitting in the booth eating dinner with a family like all of the other people were doing at the restaurant. She wanted to ride a bike, play soccer, jump on her bed, listen to her favorite songs, watch movies, she didn't want the bunny. She really wanted all of them to be away from Frank.

Angel looked at Becca, looked at her mom, looked at Ms. Mary and said, "How are you going to get Doug? When will you get my brother?"

Fammy looked at Angel and Becca, "I'm gonna be just fine. I will go get your brother and we will meet you guys later. *Maak je geen zorgen, ik zal het doen,*" she told the girls.

Fammy turned to head out of the office, Becca ran and grabbed her. "Don't leave us, don't leave us," Becca cried frantically. She wrapped her arms around Fammy and held tight.

Fammy pulled Becca off of her, and said, "I will get your brother. It will be okay."

Something about the way she said it made Angel think it wasn't what her mom wanted to do.

It was like her mom was just saying that for the officers.

Angel looked at her mom and Becca.

It wasn't right with her gut.

There wasn't any voice telling her anything.

Angel was just so tired she couldn't think right now.

She couldn't feel.

She closed her eyes, held onto the stupid stress bunny, and she went down the rabbit hole.

CHAPTER 9

THE ORPHANAGE

IT WAS LAUNDRY day, and all the girls had to line up around the bed to grab their clothes as the headmaster, Big Ann, dumped them out of the laundry basket. Angel and Becca had to wait until everyone else got their clothes, and then they were allowed to pick out their clothes for the week.

"Those are mine," said Carrie and Dawn at the same time.

"You're lying; that's mine," answered Dawn. "Your panties don't look like that, and those have flowers. They're mine."

Carrie reached across the back of Angel and hit Dawn in the back of the head. Carrie looked at Angel and said, "Why did you hit me? You ain't got no right hitting me!"

Angel looked at Carrie and said, "I didn't hit you. It was Dawn!"

As Angel was speaking, Carrie slapped Dawn again.

All of the girls standing around the bed moved back because they knew something was about to happen. Angel turned and balled up her hand just in case a fight broke out. Angel never took any crap off these girls and no one else around here should take her crap either. She and Becca had been here a couple of months after her mom left them. She knew that once you started letting them take advantage of you, then you got bullied. Angel wasn't going to have any of it. If Carrie wanted to fight she would fight her even though Carrie was twice her size.

Angel would never let anyone ever hit her again. Ever.

"Shut up, both of you! If you don't shut up, none of y'all are getting any supper or any panties to wear!" Big Ann said, and the room got quiet.

"Grab y'all's crap, and then get back to your rooms. We'll ring the bell when dinner is done. Now go on, all of y'all."

The girls started grabbing what was leftover on the bed. Angel grabbed four pairs of underwear, four shirts, and four pairs of pants, and then she tried to find a set of sheets. They were only allowed four outfits for the week because the rule was that they could wear an outfit more than once. By the time she found a complete set of sheets, all of the other girls had left. Angel picked up a raggedy old sheet that once had been white but was now some shade of light brown. She looked at it in disgust, but she was also a little grateful that she found a set. The week prior, she'd just slept on a blanket that barely covered her cot.

Big Ann was watching her the whole time pick out her clothes.

"Angel, if you want to get along with all these youngins in here, you've got to learn to shut your mouth and do your time. You and your sister ain't got nobody that's why you got community clothes and no underwear of your own. Ain't nobody got time for y'all being picky. Now I'm fixin' to write you's up for insubordination against an elder. Hurry up, girl, and get on."

Angel didn't say a word.

She hated this place, and half the time, she had no idea what Big Ann was saying. She couldn't understand her. Big Ann spoke with this huge southern accent that Angel had never heard of before like "y'all" and "fixin'."

What did all those words even mean?

She figured out real quick that "y'all" meant everyone. She was used to saying, "you guys," but not the "y'all" thing. The first time she heard it reminded her of a western she had watched on TV one time.

She thought it sounded so silly.

She still had yet to understand "fixin'." All she knew was that word meant to fix something. Big Ann used it all the time, and Angel wanted so badly to ask what was it that she was about to fix.

Angel thought it was pretty ironic because Big Ann never did anything but sit around, eat and yell at them.

Angel also figured out what the word, "youngin'" meant. She knew she was younger than some of the girls in the orphanage, but some were younger than her. And what did the "in" in the word mean? Even though there were many kids in the orphanage of all ages, Big Ann said that word to all of them. Angel never really thought that she was a "youngin'." She just thought she was just a girl.

"Whatcha' laughing at girl? Go on, go yonder to your room, ya hear?" Big Ann told Angel.

Another word to figure out. *Geez this Georgia thing is so odd,* Angel thought to herself as she gathered her clothes for the week

She walked down the end of the hall to her bedroom. It wasn't exactly her bedroom; it was a room that housed her and nine other girls. The hallway was long and bright. Angel hated the lights because they hurt her eyes, and they were on all the time, even at night.

The place reminded her of what prison might look like. She even felt like it was a prison, especially when Big Ann would make comments about her doing her time. Angel didn't do anything. Why would she need to serve time? Angel wondered how long she would do her time here. Becca seemed to get along with everyone, especially the younger kids. She would spend hours reading and playing with the toddlers or she'd play games and act out stories, which seemed really boring to Angel but it kept Becca happy.

Sometimes Angel would wake up from her regular nightmares, see the light, and think she'd died. That maybe all of this was a dream and she had actually killed herself with the knife she kept hidden under her bed.

But then she would come to her senses, and realize she was lying in a cot in the orphanage.

She would lay awake at night and worry about her mom but at the same time, she hated her. She decided she would never refer to her as her mom anymore, her name was Fammy. She didn't deserve to be her mom.

Fammy was supposed to get her brother and then leave Frank. They stayed at a protected safe house in Savannah. That lasted all of one week before Fammy got in touch with Frank.

While they were at the safe house, they had learned that Frank was wanted by the FBI for even more bad things. Angel and Becca were going to have to testify in front of a judge about the things they saw. Angel wasn't the least bit scared of doing that, she couldn't wait to tell them about that man.

But Fammy messed that up.

She told the girls that they were going on a picnic one day, and she had a surprise for them. Angel knew Fammy well—knew her mannerisms and how she acted when she was about to meet a man.

Fammy had her face painted, her tight clothes on, and her cigarette in her hand. Her face was beaming with excitement.

As they walked out the door, Angel heard it.

She heard the voice.

It said, *stand firm*. She heard it in her gut.

She knew.

Frank was back.

"Is he going to be there? Are you seeing him? Is he out of jail?" Angel said to Fammy.

Fammy bit her bottom lip, flipped her hair, and took a drag off her Salem Light cigarette. She didn't speak, she didn't even look at Angel.

"Choose. Us or him," Angel looked at Fammy with her arms across her chest and stood firm.

"What are you talking about? He has changed, he promised me. He will never touch you guys again. He didn't mean to do any of that, and he is good person. He a good person. You will see. He make it up to you. He good," Fammy pleaded with Angel to change her mind about Frank. She even suggested that everything they went through was not as bad as Angel remembered. Angel knew what Fammy was doing, if Angel and Becca could change their stories, then Frank wouldn't be charged.

Angel just couldn't believe her. What was wrong with her? She was going to choose Frank over her kids, over her.

"Choose. Us or him. That's your only option. Who is going to be?"

And then, Fammy left her and Becca. She walked out of their lives and never came back.

Fammy never returned to the safe house. And from that

moment Angel and Becca were on their own. Doug left with Fammy.

Once the safe house realized that Fammy was not coming back, they called the Department of Family and Children's Services who brought them to the orphanage.

It was just them, her and Becca.

It seemed like forever ago, but Angel tried not to think of Fammy at all. Becca swore up and down that she would come back to get them. She thought it was all a misunderstanding.

Angel knew differently. She knew in her heart that Fammy had chosen Frank over them.

They were stuck in this prison, but it sure was better than that trailer park they had all lived in with Frank.

That was the stuff that stayed with her in her nightmares.

The nightmares that always led to her escaping to her rabbit holes.

Angel finally reached her room at the end of the hallway, quietly made her way to her cot. She dumped her clothes and began to unfold them. The rule was that they had to fold their clothes and put them on the shelves labeled with their name.

"You better watch your back, girl. We gonna get you," Carrie yelled from the other end of the room. All the other girls in the room started laughing and giggling, except for Becca. Becca's bed was right by Angel's, and she whispered to Angel.

"It's not worth it, Angel. Let it go, you know she is just going to make things worse for you if you respond."

Angel looked at her sister and glared. Angel wished Becca would shut up; she always wanted peace. Angel didn't feel peace—she wanted to hit someone, break out, fight back, move, anything but make peace. She hated this place, she hated Carrie, and all Angel wanted to do was hit her. Angel looked across the room at Carrie and tried to think of something to say. She had to do something so that they didn't see her as weak or afraid.

Just then, a loud bell rang to let the girls know it was time for dinner. All the girls waited until Carrie went first because none of them wanted to have watched their back as they walked through the hallways with no adults present.

Lots could happen in the hallways.

Becca and Angel were the last to leave the room.

"Just be quiet and don't say anything, Angel," Becca said as they walked down the hall.

"I can't help it; she bosses everyone around all the time. She isn't better than anyone. This orphanage is awful, she is awful, and I don't want to be here," Angel responded.

"Well, I like it and I don't want any trouble, so please be quiet and good. Mom is coming to get us soon. We just have to wait this out," Becca put her arm around Angel reassuringly.

Angel let her, even though she hated when Becca tried to act like an older sister. but she knew that Fammy was not coming back, not now or anytime soon.

She wished Becca would stop calling Fammy "mom."

Fammy was not a mom, and there was no way that Angel would ever let Becca go with her. She would die before that would happen.

CHAPTER 10

ISLAND OF HOPE

As THE DAYS turned into months, Angel had gotten a lot taller and she had gained some weight. None of the clothes she picked out on the weekly laundry picks fit her anymore.

Angel and Becca had started school again, and their case-worker had gotten them some glasses, which Angel hated.

They were horrible, thick, and ugly.

Big Ann would make her wear them every morning as she ate breakfast and loaded the bus.

"You wear them glasses, Angel. Waste of money for you not to wear them. They ugly fo sure, but you wear them," and then she would laugh at Angel.

Angel hated wearing them, and she would hide them once they got on the school bus.

Angel didn't really like her school, and she was placed in all the remedial classes again. She was trying really hard to show her teachers that she didn't need to be in those classes.

She wanted to go far away one day, far away from this orphanage and far away from Georgia.

She dreamt of changing her name.

THE BOOK OF ANGEL

She hated her name. Who was named Angel?

She wasn't pretty like a real Angel, definitely not angelic or peaceful.

Fammy messed up real bad when she named Angel, but then again, Fammy messed up a whole lot of things.

One day after school, Angel and Becca stepped off the school bus and walked into the orphanage with the rest of the children with no parents.

Big Ann walked up to Angel and Becca and said, "Your case manager is here to talk with y'all. Angel, don't you be running that mouth either, ya hear?"

Angel opened her mouth, but before she could speak, her caseworker said, "Hey, you guys, come over here and sit awhile," and Angel decided not to say anything.

She just glared at Big Ann and walked away, but she made sure that Big Ann saw her glaring.

Big Ann was a large woman with hands to match, that shook when she pointed. Her shoulder-length brown hair desperately needed a haircut and a good washing. She also needed a good teeth cleaning. She had the biggest butt Angel had ever seen. Sometimes just to fit the doors at the orphanage, Big Ann had to turn sideways.

"How are y'all doing? Becca, how is school going? I know you were having some trouble in your math classes?"

"Well, I am trying but it is hard. I try really hard," Becca replied.

Angel sat down with her arms crossed.

This is a waste of time, Angel thought. *A complete waste of time.*

Angel didn't need a caseworker telling her how to do classwork.

Angel's caseworker was a small African American woman

named Candy. She looked like she was still a teenager. She had perfect teeth and had a bright yellow sheer shirt with a black skirt. Angel always thought her caseworker was pretty and very fashionable, if fashion was someone's thing.

"Angel what about you? How are things going?" Candy said it in an over-exaggeratedly nice tone, hoping to get a response from Angel.

Angel looked at Candy and muttered the word "fine."

"Um, well that's good. I have some news that I would like to share with you both. So, the state has decided that since your mom–"

Angel interrupted, "Fammy, her name is Fammy, not mom."

"Okay, well, uh, Fammy has been gone for a while, they… the state feels that you two should be placed into foster care," Candy explained.

Angel looked Candy up and down.

Candy went on, "Well, um, we have found a foster home for you guys. And we think that it is a really good fit. You two can be together, which is really hard to find a home that both of y'all can go together, and the family has other teenage girls, too."

Angel just looked at the caseworker with a blank stare.

Becca sat up in her chair.

"Does that mean our mom can't come back and get us?" Becca asked.

Angel just rolled her eyes.

God, why does Becca keep thinking that? She is not coming back.

"No of course not. When your mom returns, if she returns, we will look at all of that and see where things are at that point.

Right now, we just think this home is a really good placement for you guys," Candy said.

Liar, Angel said to herself. *Liar, liar, pants on fire.*

Everything anyone said was a lie. Every time people said that things were going to be good, Angel had to expect the opposite. This would be no different.

"So, this is a big announcement and a change for you both, but your foster mom will be here in about an hour to get you. What do you think? Angel, what do you think?" Candy anxiously looked at Angel.

Angel glared at Candy the caseworker.

Candy looked back and smiled reassuringly.

"Well what do you think? Candy asked again.

Trust me.

Angel winced when she heard it.

She had not heard the voice in months.

Trust me.

Angel unfolded her arms.

Candy saw Angel's demeanor change a little, and she smiled.

"So, you guys think you can gather your stuff, and be ready?"

Becca looked at Angel for her approval.

Angel didn't really know where this was going, but she heard the voice, and if that was her gut, then she could listen to it, maybe a little.

"Okay," said Angel.

"Great, and I'll go ahead and make the call to let her know to be here and get all your paperwork ready."

Angel and Becca got up, and Candy went and told Big Ann that they would be leaving for a new home.

Angel heard the word home come out of Candy's mouth. Home.

Angel didn't know what that word meant to her case-worker, but to Angel, it meant a lot of things.

Uncertainty.

Fear.

Anxiety.

Hope.

Did Angel feel hope?

Angel and Becca gathered their stuff, which took all of ten minutes. It wasn't like they had anything anyway. They didn't have suitcases or bags. They were given a black trash bag, which they shared.

Angel, Becca, and Candy sat by the orphanage door in the family visiting area waiting on their foster parent to come pick them up.

Angel and Becca had never used this room because no family had ever come to visit them, and now here they were waiting on their new adventure.

To Angel, waiting felt like an eternity. She tried hard not to show any emotion to her caseworker. She didn't want her to know anything about her. She had all kinds of thoughts entering her mind.

Most of all, she was trying so hard to stay in the moment and not go down her rabbit hole.

She saw Becca keep looking out the orphanage window.

"Stop Becca. You are getting on my nerves!" Angel finally told her.

Angel hoped that this new home thing would be good for Becca. Becca deserved it. Becca was always nice to people and always trying to make people happy. Not like Angel.

"A black long car just drove up. Is that her?" Becca said.

Before Angel could catch herself, she looked out the window. Yep, there was a black car out there. A really nice car.

She watched this woman walk toward the front of the orphanage.

She was not short, not tall, a little overweight.

She had dark hair.

She was dressed nice.

She had a purse on her arm, a large purse.

She didn't look anything like Fammy.

Angel turned her head around and sat back in her chair.

Here we go.

Candy walked toward the door and opened it for the woman.

"Hello, Linda. Thank you so much for getting here today so fast. You are going to love the girls," she said as she ushered the woman toward Angel and Becca.

Angel made eye contact with Linda. Linda looked back at her. Their eyes locked.

Angel looked away.

"I'm Linda. You're Becca?" she said as she looked at Angel.

Angel shook her head with an adamant shake of the head, no.

"I'm Becca. I'm the oldest," and Becca jumped up to greet Linda.

Angel rolled her eyes; this was not starting out good.

"Oh, okay, so you're Angel?" she looked at Angel again.

Angel didn't look up. She nodded her head yes.

"Well, let's get your things, and we'll get you guys out of here," said Candy.

Linda looked around, "Where are your things?"

Angel said, "This is it. This amazing black trash bag, full of treasure."

Linda said, "Okay, well that's okay. It's okay. We can add to the treasure eventually," and she grabbed the black trash bag.

They headed out the door, and Angel looked back.

She saw Big Ann glaring at her.

Angel glared back.

But this time, Angel made sure she smiled at Big Ann. A big, fat sarcastic smile that would match her big, fat sarcastic butt.

"Have you guys had dinner yet," Linda asked the girls as she opened up the car door.

Dinner? Why would Linda ask if they had dinner? Of course, they hadn't had dinner. It was 12:00 in the afternoon, nobody eats dinner at noon. Angel was kind of worried about this Linda lady. Who eats dinner this early?

"No, we haven't had dinner," Angel said and sat down in the back seat, letting Becca sit in the front. She really didn't want to be that close to Linda anyway.

"Well good, because I know this really good place named the Wienerschnitzel. Do y'all like hotdogs? I love hotdogs," Linda said.

The last time Angel had hot dogs was in the stolen car and she got hit in the mouth for asking questions, so Angel decided to just shake her head. *I guess we'll eat dinner at noon, maybe that's what this family does? Weird.*

Linda put an eight-track tape into the stereo player, and some strange music that Angel had never heard of came on.

They drove through the streets of Savannah, Georgia. Angel noticed how pretty the streets looked, especially since it was spring. Lots of beautiful red, pink, and white flowers lined the streets.

They drove into the parking lot of the Wienerschnitzel and Linda ordered them hotdogs and a coke. The coke thing was new for Angel. In California, Angel always drank pop or juice, she never even heard of coke.

As Angel drank her coke and ate her hotdog, she listened to the song that was playing on the radio. She always loved to listen to music, she hadn't had a radio to listen to in forever, well not since her days of living in California or the nightmare with Frank.

Yeah, she liked this song.

She looked at the windows, eating her hotdog.

"Um, Linda, um Ms. Linda. What is this song? Who sings it?

"Just call me Linda. Johnny Cash. He is a country singer, and it is country music. Haven't you ever heard of country?" Linda said as she looked through the rearview mirror at Angel.

"No, never have."

"You like it?" Linda asked Angel.

Angel paused before she spoke. She couldn't let Linda know she liked it.

"It's alright," she shrugged her shoulders.

Linda looked back at Angel and Angel met her eyes for the second time that day. Angel looked away.

"Where are we going? What kind of house do you live in?" Becca chatted away as they continued driving.

Angel tuned her sister out. Savannah was a big place, Angel observed. They had already been driving for a good while, even though they did stop for a hotdog, they were still driving.

"Well, we live in a home that is on an island. Savannah is full of islands. They aren't big islands, and sometimes you don't really feel like you are on one because every island is connected to the main part of Savannah through causeways, which are like small bridges," Linda talked.

Angel listened, but she didn't act like she was. Savannah sounded a lot different than California. Nobody lived on islands, they rode city buses and stayed in hotels, they didn't visit islands.

"I have lived in Savannah my whole life, and just got remarried a couple of months ago. I have kept foster kids for the past couple of years. All teenage girls, just like you," Linda turned down a small road.

Yeah, no, thought Angel. *You have never kept a kid like me,* she said to herself as she kept looking at the window. She saw a glimpse of water and a bridge.

"Are we here?" Becca asked.

"Almost, we have one more small causeway and then we will reach the island we live on." Linda said.

Angel saw all kinds of wet, marshy-looking grass. It was actually kind of pretty, in a different way. She saw a white seagull fly away, and before she realized she was smiling.

Angel finally decided to speak and asked, "What is the name of the island that you live on?"

Linda looked at Angel in the back seat and said, "It's named Isle of Hope. It was given the name a long time ago. People, colonists would come here trying to escape Yellow Fever. People believed they could come to the island and be healed. There are a lot of interesting historical sites around the island, and of course Savannah. You'd be surprised at how much history is around this city."

Isle of Hope.

What a name for an island, Angel thought. Maybe hope could be found on an island. Maybe…

And Angel watched as the big black car drove into the driveway. This was now her new home.

CHAPTER 11

ROLLING EYES

ANGEL OPENED THE door to the house, and noticed the carpet had been vacuumed.

That meant that Linda was cleaning. When Linda cleans, Angel always gets into trouble because she never cleans like Linda wants her to.

"Girls? Is that y'all? Linda yelled from behind her giant vacuum cleaner. Linda turned off the vacuum.

"Yeah, we're home Mom!" Jennifer yelled back as she took off her shoes and put them on the shoe shelf by the door.

"It's us. We took our shoes off," Julie followed Jennifer.

Angel hated taking off her shoes. But she did.

Linda appeared and looked at Angel sternly.

Angel knew she had done something from the look Linda was giving her.

Here it comes, Angel said to herself, as she was trying to figure out what she had done or not done.

"Angel, your room is a disaster, again. Your clothes are everywhere. It's disgusting. So you, young lady, are grounded for the weekend. I want you to go straight upstairs and clean that room!"

"But I have tons of homework. I'm also supposed to spend the night out this weekend, remember? I can't be grounded. I'll clean it up I promise, just let me go this weekend," Angel pleaded.

"Just clean your room, Angel. Dang, all you have to do is stop making messes," piped in Jennifer from behind Linda.

"I'm so hungry. What do we have for snacks?" Jennifer walked toward the kitchen and opened the pantry door.

Jennifer was Linda's daughter. Her *real* daughter as Angel calls her. Jennifer was always putting her opinion into everyone's business.

Angel glared at Jennifer and walked toward the steps leading to the upstairs.

"Go clean your room and please, stop rolling your eyes!" Linda said to Angel.

God, Angel wished Linda would just shut up and leave her alone.

She never quits. On and on about everything.

Angel stomped upstairs.

Linda was always on her case, constantly telling her what to do.

Angel never did anything right.

Never. Angel could make straight As, work four days a week, and yet she would find something to complain about. She couldn't wait until she turned eighteen and headed to college. She wasn't sure which college yet, but she was going somewhere far away from her and this foster home. She and Becca had been living with John and Linda for almost three years since the orphanage. Angel was fifteen now and college seemed like it was just around the corner for her. She had already started looking at where she wanted to go.

Angel opened up the door to her room and tripped over two piles of clothes.

Who cares if my room is dirty? It is mine anyway.

Angel sat on her bed. God, she hated this bedspread. All the stupid bunnies running in mid-air trying to get somewhere. Linda had picked it out because it was on sale. Along time ago, rabbits and bunnies were important to Angel, but the older she got they just seemed stupid.

She bent down to pick up the shirt on the first pile of clothes and started to go through it.

Jennifer opened the door.

"God, don't you ever knock?" Angel yelled at Jennifer.

"No, but can I borrow the shirt you just bought at the mall?" Jennifer casually leaned against the doorframe.

"No, you can't borrow my shirt. I haven't even worn it yet" Angel scoffed.

"Come on, let me wear it. I'll stop calling you Amazon woman if you do." One of Jennifer's superpowers was bargaining.

"If I let you borrow the shirt, will you leave me alone?"

"Yes. So can I wear it?" Jennifer was already walking over the pile of clothes to get to Angel's closet.

"Tell you what…you can wear this one," Angel threw her work shirt that was on the floor at Jennifer's feet. As a waitress at Ryan's steakhouse, her clothes got pretty dirty.

"Oh my God! This reeks of nasty sweat and steak juice. No wonder Mom got so mad at you. This smells so bad," Jennifer gagged dramatically.

"Let me borrow it, please. I want to wear it to church tonight," she pleaded again.

Angel rolled her eyes. "Fine, take it. But you have to talk to Linda about ungrounding me."

"Oh yeah. You got invited to that party, didn't you?" Jennifer moved closer to the closet searching for the shirt then turned back to Angel. "Okay, I will but she won't listen to me. You know how she is about stuff. She grounded me last week for my grades."

Angel got up, pushed Jennifer to the side, and got the shirt. It still had tags on it.

"Here, don't mess it up," Angel handed it to Jennifer.

"Yes! Thank you, I won't mess it up. Promise!" Jennifer grabbed the shirt and left the room.

Angel sat back down on the bed.

Jennifer was the perfect daughter. She was short and petite, quiet, and fair skinned.

Angel was far from perfect—tall and big, loud, weird olive-looking skin, and moles everywhere. Even one on her face by her nose.

Jennifer was blonde, wore a size 2, or maybe even smaller. Jennifer even had small feet.

Angel had ugly brown hair, wore bigger clothes, and had the biggest feet in the family, even bigger than John.

She hated the way she looked.

Everybody liked Jennifer. Everyone hated Angel.

Jennifer was shy, but Angel was never afraid to speak up when she thought things were wrong. In fact, it was a running joke in the family that Linda would always yell Angel's name first if she was trying to find out who did something. She started with, "An–" and then would quickly change it to Jennifer, Becca, or Julie. So it always sounded as if she was saying Aunt Becca, Aunt Jennifer, or Aunt Julie. Julie had just moved into the house a couple of months ago, but it was still always Angel whose was the first name to be called. It wasn't always

Angel's fault, it was just because Angel was always busy and always involved with something...generally making messes.

Angel knew that in her heart, she was really just jealous of Jennifer. She was jealous that Jennifer had everything that she wished she had, and it wasn't Jennifer's fault. Jennifer had her faults but she tried to be nice, except for the times she called Angel an Amazon woman.

Angel looked around her room, it was kind of messy.

She picked up another shirt and folded it. She picked up another shirt, it was dirty, she put it in the dirty clothes basket. She sorted a few more clothes, and was making some progress, until she finally saw her bedroom floor.

Go Angel, go Angel, she said to herself.

She moved toward the pile that needed to be hung up in the closet. She reached for a hanger and hung the blouse on the plastic hanger. Just as she was about to hang it in her closet, she heard heavy footsteps. Those were Linda's steps, hard and heavy.

Linda opened Angel's door

Why couldn't she knock? thought Angel

Angel froze with her back toward the door of her bedroom as she waited for Linda to criticize her, again.

"Angel, we are going to eat before church tonight. Can you please come help to set the table in about an hour? Unless you want to come now? Everyone is going to watch a little TV downstairs before dinner," Linda said at the doorway.

Angel noticed that Linda's tone had changed, it didn't sound as angry as earlier and it was much softer, but Angel was still mad at her for grounding her.

Without turning around, Angel said, "I really have too much to do. Do I have to go to church? I have got so much homework and I have been busy cleaning my room so I haven't even started. I have a paper due tomorrow and I still need to type it."

"Can you turn around to speak to me before we talk about all of that?" Linda asked to Angel's back.

Angel did not want to turn around. She really did not want to engage with Linda anymore today. She rolled her eyes, lifted her neck back, sighed heavily and turned her body around toward Linda but she refused to make eye contact.

"Well can I.? Stay home?" Angel said to Linda without looking at her.

Angel could feel the tension between them, and she was pretty sure Linda felt it too. There was always tension between them.

After an awkward silence, Linda finally responded.

"Angel, I really think it is important for us to spend time as a family. Eating dinner together and attending church is part of that. I know you are busy, but attending youth group is important. You might not see that now, but one day you will. But when we get back I will help you type your paper. Good Lord, you know you can't type. I don't know why you didn't sign up for typing class instead of yearbook class. You need to learn to type before you head to college…" She signed and rubbed her hands gently down the front of her dress. "But… we will discuss whether or not you can go out this weekend later," Linda said all of this as if she had been rehearsing what to say to Angel.

Angel raised her eyes a little bit. She heard Linda say that they would discuss if she could go this weekend. But she also heard her say she knew Angel wanted to go to college. How did she know that? Was she going through her things? Did she read Angel's diary?

Why did she have to always pick apart everything that

Angel did? Angel loves her yearbook class; she was really good at it too. Who wants to learn to type? Yuck, none of her friends were in typing class anyway.

"Okay, Angel?" Linda prompted.

"Okay, okay," Angel replied

Linda turned and headed back down the stairs.

Angel didn't know how to read Linda. She just couldn't figure her out sometimes. One minute Linda was nice to her, and then the next she was mean. It was so hard to figure out where Angel stood with her. Linda always had this idea of what their family should look like, but Angel just didn't fit in with that idea.

Angel picked up a pair of shorts and put them in her dresser drawer.

She wondered why Linda always wanted all the girls to look a certain way, to look "polished" she would say.

Angel was so much taller than all of them, she looked hideous in bows, shoulder pads, and ruffles.

All of them looked cute, but not Angel.

Angel looked like an Amazon woman. Jennifer gave her that nickname because she was so much taller than everyone else.

Angel saw a pair of pants under her bed. She moved the bedspread to get to the pants.

She hated this bedspread.

Jennifer got to pick out her bedspread, and it was pink. Jennifer's room reminded her of the movie *Pretty in Pink*. That fit Jennifer for sure.

Angel loved that movie.

She put the pants on a hanger she had found on the floor.

She wished that she could have a life like Molly Ringwald, even if they forgot her birthday. At least she had a real family.

Even when Linda introduced her to people, she said, "This is Jennifer," and then she said, "these are my foster daughters, Angel, Becca, and Julie."

Then the conversation was always about Jennifer.

Angel would just stand there stood there and listened to how great Jennifer is, blah, blah, blah. Most of the time, the conversations were always at church because they went there all the time. Like all the time. Linda's sister went there, too, and so did her friends.

And Linda had lots of church friends, and when they headed to church that evening, they would probably be there too.

They all dressed the same way: pantyhose, freshly ironed shirts, red lipstick, and heels. All of them looked like they just stepped out of 1955.

All Angel wanted was to be part of a regular family and not to have to constantly tell people she was a foster kid, and not part of some 50s fantasy.

It was so embarrassing. None of her friends were foster kids.

Why couldn't she just be normal?

Living in a foster home is not normal.

There had been others in the home. One girl got pregnant and left. Linda had a fit over that. She went on and on about how Christians don't have sex before marriage and good girls don't do that. Angel knew that if she ever got pregnant before she got married, that would be the end of her living there for sure. Linda was not going to have a pregnant girl living in her house. She didn't think John would care; he just did whatever Linda told him to do. It reminded her of the show *Little House on the Prairie* and the relationship between Nells and Mrs. Olsen.

Linda told John what to do, when to do it, and how high she wanted him to jump! That was definitely the relationship Linda had with John.

Angel picked up the last shirt from the pile on the floor. She should give this shirt to Jennifer, it looked better on her anyway.

As she walked down the hallway to gift the shirt, she could hear Jennifer and Julie in their room laughing.

Angel walked down the hallway of the two-story home that Linda and John had built. It was a beautiful home, Angel loved the way the wood would shine on the stair banisters.

Maybe one day she could have a home like this, maybe.

She walked by Becca's room, and didn't see her. *She must be downstairs already,* Angel thought. Poor Becca, she had really struggled this year in school.

Where Angel is always getting into trouble for stupid stuff like talking back, not cleaning her room, talking on the phone, Becca gets in trouble for her grades.

She had a hard time in school. Linda sat up with her sometimes all night, trying to get her to understand Math. She gets her numbers mixed up or something. Angel didn't think Becca liked school all that much.

Angel loved high school. She enjoyed her classes, her teachers and she had lots of friends. She loved her friends, mostly because she hung out with the athletes and cheerleaders, even though she was neither.

She wanted to be, but she had to work a part-time job. Working gave her money and independence to be able to go out with her friends on the weekend. Work gave Angel time away from this smothering house with all of its rules.

She bought the shirt she was giving to Jennifer from her last paycheck.

Angel walked into Jennifer and Julie's room.

"Hey, you want this shirt?" Angel threw the shirt on the bed toward Jennifer.

"Let me see it," Jennifer said.

"Do you want the shirt or not? It isn't a hard question," Angel stood in the doorway.

"Yeah, I'll take it. Didn't you just buy it?" Jennifer looked at Angel with her one eyebrow raised.

Jennifer had spent weeks learning how to do that. She would ask all of them if they could tell she was raising one eyebrow. Angel thought it was silly that she was trying to learn how to raise one eyebrow, like it was an important task to have in life.

Angel shrugged.

"Sure. Hey, so we were thinking this weekend we could all watch that new scary movie, *Nightmare on Elm Street,* the second one. We could pop some popcorn and hang out in the playroom," Jennifer said as she and Julie flipped pages of a magazine.

Angel moved closer to the girls, and sat down on Jennifer's bed.

She loved the color of Jennifer's room.

"Well, come on. You haven't hung out with us in a while, since you got a job. It'll be fun," Jennifer punched Angel in the arm jokingly.

"Hmmm, I have to look at my work schedule and I am also supposed to go to that party," Angel replied.

"Okay, but y'all remember the last time we did that, we all got yelled at by your mom because you started screaming at 1:30 in the morning," Julie pointed at Jennifer.

"Yeah, Jennifer you freaked out because you thought the red and green thing fell off the dresser, and it was the color of Freddie Krueger. Oh my God, that was so funny," Angel said.

"Shut up, it was scary and I saw it move. I did. It was moving" replied Jennifer.

Angel and Julie looked at each other and shook their heads.

"It never moved!" Angel and Julie said in unison.

"Let's head downstairs, we got to set the table before my mom goes crazy. You know how she gets," Jennifer got up.

"I can't, I still have to clean my room," Angel got up to head back to her room.

"You need some help?" Julie asked Angel.

"Nah, I got it. I am the messy one remember?" Angel said as she walked closer to the door to head back to her room.

"Well, don't be messy and you wouldn't have that problem. Hurry up and join us downstairs Amazon woman!" Angel heard Jennifer say loudly.

Angel walked back to her room.

She stopped at her mirror.

Was she an Amazon woman?

She had curly brown hair that she had just gotten permed, it was actually Linda's idea.

Linda said that she thought Angel's hair would look great with a perm because it was long and thick.

She could still smell the perm.

She also saw her curves beginning to form. She always heard Linda say that Angel was a "late bloomer," whatever that meant. Angel knew she was already taller than everyone else so she definitely didn't want to get any taller for sure, but if she could develop some curves, well that would be nice.

She was hoping that her hair would be good to go by this weekend because she wanted so badly to go to that party. She and her best friend were invited, of course, there would be alcohol there and she couldn't wait. Hanging out with her friends from school and work was about the only thing she liked to do, and it got her away from this house that always felt like a box.

Angel had a lot of friends, especially boys.

Angel didn't think she was all that pretty, definitely not as pretty as Jennifer. But boys were starting to pay her attention. She looked in the mirror.

Who did she look like?

Her dad?

Fammy?

Yuck Fammy.

She didn't want to look like her at all.

She could remember brushing her mom's long thick auburn hair and thinking how pretty she was. But that was long ago.

She also hadn't heard from her older brother, Doug. She had no idea what happened to them.

But right now, she didn't have time to think about them.

She had to finish the room, get ready for church, and set the stupid table.

Angel walked toward her clock radio and turned it on. Her favorite song was on, "Let's Hear it for The Boys."

She loved that song, she turned it up louder, and started to hang up the last of the pile. She made her bed and put up all her makeup from the dresser.

Angel stayed focused, she was going to clean her room, and do what she needed to do so she could go to that party. She was not going to go down any rabbit holes this time.

Angel worked as fast as she could, and didn't hear Linda yelling from the bottom of the stairs. She also didn't hear Linda walk up the stairs and come to her door,

"Angel! Angel! Turn that down! I have been yelling over that for ten minutes," Linda said as she walked into Angel's room and toward the clock radio to turn it down.

"Oh, um, sorry, I really didn't realize how loud it was. I was just trying to get this done," Angel responded to Linda.

Linda looked around the room.

Angel looked around her room too. It was clean.

"Wow, you got it cleaned up didn't ya?" Linda nodded her head in approval and a smile

Angel looked around her room again. It did look pretty good, and she was kind of proud of herself.

"All right, well you have done enough, for now. Let's go eat. Table has already been set by Jennifer and Julie. Becca had to work," Linda said as she turned to head back down the stairs.

Angel stood still.

Linda turned back, and said, "Are you coming? Come on, let's go eat. I made your favorite, pork chops and potatoes."

Angel nodded her head up and down.

She started to walk through her doorway, and out of the corner of her eye she saw something that stood out to her. The bunny print on the bedspread was wrinkled making the bunny look like he was all squished up. That bothered her. She reached out her hand and straighten out the spread. The bunny was now running in mid air like he was designed to do.

Then Angel left her room, and followed Linda down the stairs to eat her favorite dinner.

CHAPTER 12

JOSH

HE SAT DOWN in front of her. Angel tapped his shoulder.

"What is your name?" Angel asked the boy with short blond hair, while she smacked her gum. She thought he was kind of cute, in a nerdy way. Josh had a pair of glasses on, and a light blue collared shirt with a pocket. All he needed was a pen in that pocket, and he could have starred in the movie, *Revenge of the Nerds*. But he also had this sporty look, like he was trying to not look like a jock. He was something different for sure.

Angel tapped his shoulder again, "Hey, what's your name?"

The boy turned around and said, "Leave me alone."

Angel thought what a weird response. She just asked his name, why was he acting like that?

So, she tapped his shoulder again.

"Okay, so tell me your name and I'll leave you alone," Angel said again.

"Angel, stop talking. Do your work, and spit out your gum," Mrs. Ready told Angel.

Angel looked at Mrs. Ready and said, "Mrs. Ready, I was just asking his name. Since he's new and I was going to talk with him to see if he needed any help getting around the school. So I really wasn't talking. I was actually asking a question. You are always telling us that we should question things, right?"

Angel looked at Mrs. Ready and smiled.

How she loved Mrs. Ready. She was a big African American lady, and probably Angel's favorite teacher, besides Miss Rowe from a long time ago. Mrs. Ready was everyone's favorite teacher. She always had a way of making her students feel special. The whole class started laughing at what Angel had said.

Mrs. Ready took her finger and pushed her glasses up to her face. Mrs. Ready's glasses were always resting on her nose. Angel waited for Mrs. Ready's iconic words. She would look at her students with her glasses on her nose, lift her chin down and say, "Now class, let's get settled."

Mrs. Ready looked at Angel, and then at the class and said it. "Class, now class let's get settled. Angel, please stop bothering that boy. Come up to my desk."

Angel got up out of her seat and walked up to Mrs. Ready. She knew she wasn't in trouble, but she also knew Mrs. Ready would have something wise and witty to say to her. Mrs. Ready always made Angel feel as if she was smart, wanted, and valued. Mrs. Ready made Angel feel as if she could be and say anything she wanted. Mrs. Ready always had a huge box fan blowing at her face because it was so hot in the Savannah classrooms without air conditioning, and sometimes walking up to Mrs. Ready's desk was like walking into a wind tunnel. On hot days it was a relief, but most of the time, Angel tried really hard to put her back to the fan so her hair wouldn't get messed up. She spent hours spraying and teasing her hair in the morning, and the last thing she needed was for her hair to get messed up.

Angel approached her desk, and strategically stood with her back to the fan.

Mrs. Ready looked at Angel and said in a low deep voice, "Miss Angel, you are a lady, a beautiful lady. Treat yourself like a lady, act like a lady. Don't bother that boy. Use all that energy to write this poem here that you need to write for your grade. You hear me?'

Angel said, "Yes"

"Yes, what?" asked Mrs. Ready to Angel.

Angel looked at Mrs. Ready. "Ma'am? Yes, Ma'am?"

Angel still couldn't get used to saying this ma'am thing. When she'd lived in California, nobody said that word. Linda always made her say it back. She didn't mind it as much now, but it still felt really strange.

Angel turned and started to walk back to her seat.

"Angel?" said Mrs. Ready.

Angel turned around to see Mrs. Ready motion for her to walk back to her desk.

Mrs. Ready pushed her glasses back on her nose and whispered to Angel, "His name is Joshua. He just moved here from Tybee. Be nice to him. He is special. It could be a good thing." Mrs. Ready straightened the rabbit paper clip holder on her desk and flashed an encouraging smile.

Angel smiled real big back.

She had no idea what she meant about it could be a good thing, but whatever, she knew his name, and that was all she wanted. His name was Joshua, probably Josh for short.

She would call him Josh.

As the school year progressed, Angel and Josh had several classes together. Angel noticed that Josh began waiting for her in the morning time when she arrived at school. She never had a boy wait for her. Josh was more than considerate, he was kind, compassionate toward others, and well liked by everyone.

One day, Angel decided that she would ask Josh if she could wear his jersey for the Pep Rally. It was a tradition that the girls ask the football players for their jersey to wear on Spirit Day.

Angel was very confident that Josh would say yes, so she was surprised that Josh told her no, she could not wear his jersey.

Angel overheard Josh talking to his friends Bradley and Conner while she watched him at practice that afternoon.

"Why did you tell Angel she couldn't wear your jersey? She is the finest girl in this school, and you told her no?" Bradley and Conner shook their heads as they walked to the baseball field.

"You told her no, bro. You said NO to the hottest girl in the school!" Conner hit Josh in the arm.

Josh glanced at Angel and lowered his voice, but she could still hear him.

"She scares me a little. It is like every time I am around her, I can't think. She is so different than any girl I have ever known. I can't explain it," Josh said as he carried his bat bag.

"Well, if that was my decision, that chick would be wearing my jersey. Today," said Bradley. He glanced up to where Angel sat and winked at her.

"Yeah, you need to rethink that," Conner said.

"Lets go boys on the field!" Coach Webb yelled. Bradley, Conner, and Josh ran toward the field as fast as they could. Coach Webb never played when it came to being at practice on time. If you were late, the whole team ran.

Angel left after the boys warmed up. Her heart pulled at

her with his decision. Maybe she should just move on and try to lose interest in him, but she wasn't sure she could. Josh was different, too. She may have felt rejected, but at least she knew that Josh liked her. She tried not to go down her rabbit hole.

Angel got in her car and started her drive home in the car that Linda and John had helped her buy. It was a Chevy Spectrum. Angel loved her little car. She cranked up the music when she heard "Funky Cold Medina" by Tone Loc. She got lost in the lyrics and her thoughts as she made her way home. When she arrived home, she went to her room to do homework. She had to work on her research paper and do her math work.

Angel worked hard on her homework for over two hours, when she heard the phone ring. She didn't answer it in her room hoping someone would answer it downstairs. She was almost finished.

"Angel it's for you," said Becca from down the hallway in her bedroom.

"For me? Who is it?" Angel asked, she wasn't expecting any phone calls.

"I think he said his name was Josh," Becca said smiling. She knew how Angel felt about Josh.

Angel's face broke out into a smile.

"Okay, I got it in my room. Hang it up!," she yelled back.

Angel had the phone in her hand. It was Josh.

"Josh? Hey, how was practice?," Angel said into the phone with the cord wrapped around her neck from where she scrambled to answer the phone and didn't untangle it fast enough.

"It was good, so I was wondering if you still wanted to wear my jersey?," Josh said over the phone.

Angel could not stop smiling and replied "Well, what took you so long to say yes?,"

CHAPTER 13

HOMECOMING QUEEN

ANGEL WAS GETTING ready for Homecoming. It was only 1:00 in the afternoon.

She was so excited for tonight she could hardly sleep the night before

She had been nominated for Homecoming Court. She couldn't believe it when they announced her name at school a few weeks ago. She would never have thought that she would have even been nominated.

Her, a foster kid, on Homecoming Court?

Josh, her boyfriend, told Angel that he asked all of his friends to vote for her. God, how she loved Josh. They had just started dating this year, but she already knew that there was something so special about him. She was in a horrible relationship with another guy last school year, and she thought he really loved her. She wanted him to love her, but he wanted her to be something she wasn't.

Every time they were together, she drifted into her rabbit holes.

ANGIE BOWEN

She would try really hard not to when she was with him, but she always did.

He was infatuated with how Angel looked and wanted Angel to look like the girl from the video made by Whitesnake, "Here I Go Again." When they would go out on dates, he would specifically ask her to wear tight skirts, short skirts, and low-cut shirts. Angel hated dressing like that.

It reminded her of how Fammy used to dress.

But she thought she'd loved him. Women were supposed to please their men. At least that's what Fammy used to say.

Linda had a different opinion. She said that real women should be confident in who they are, not in who they are with. Linda was always telling her and her foster sisters, to stand up straight, hold their heads high, and always always wear clean underwear.

Linda said if they were ever in a wreck and had to go to the hospital, nobody would think bad about her girls because they had clean underwear. Every time she said that all of the girls would laugh.

But Angel didn't have to dress up for Josh. He was different.

He didn't care if she wore makeup or wore jogging pants. He just didn't focus on the things she wore, he focused on her, and of course baseball.

And football. And, well, any sports.

But tonight, she wanted to dress up for him, she had picked out a red dress to wear for Homecoming Court. Josh wouldn't see her until after the game, because he would be in the locker room during halftime. She wanted him to see her in this dress. She thought she looked amazing. It was a little tight, but it showed off her curves.

Her escort, Jamie, one of her best friends, would be wearing a suit. Most of the girls on the court had their dads to escort them, but Angel really didn't have a dad. She knew that John probably didn't want to be her escort, so she asked Jamie to be her escort instead. Jamie seemed excited. He really didn't have any girlfriends; he was a little different. Angel secretly thought he was gay. She didn't care. She and Jamie did everything together. Jamie couldn't play football because he had a heart condition, but he did play baseball. He also hung out with her, Josh, and their friends, but during football season, it was just her and Jamie.

Angel spent the rest of the afternoon getting ready, and before she knew it, she heard Jennifer yelling, "Hey, stupid! Your date is here."

Angel rolled her eyes, and yelled back, "I'm almost done."

She put on a last swipe of red lipstick and walked down the steps.

As she turned the corner, she saw Linda, John, Jennifer, and her other sisters with their coats and purses. Jamie stood awkwardly by the door.

Angel had to do a double-take, why did they have their coats and stuff ready? Were they going?

"Angel, you look really pretty," said Linda.

"You look really nice," said John.

"She's alright. Let's go so we don't have to sit with a bunch of losers," Jennifer said as she was walking toward the door.

Angel was a little puzzled, she had no idea that any of them were coming. She hadn't really talked about it, and actually, she didn't even know that they knew about it.

"Um, this is Jamie, you guys remember, Jamie?" Angel said to Linda and John.

Linda looked at Jamie, "Isn't your dad Glenn?"

Jamie, who looked really uncomfortable, said, "Yes, yes, ma'am"

"Yeah, I dated your dad in high school. Hope he is doing well. We had some wild times for sure. Tell him I said hey."

Angel's mouth dropped, *this night keeps weirder and weirder,* "Um, okay, well we are going to go, and we will see you guys at the game."

Angel and Jamie finally made it to the car and shut the door.

"What the? Like what?" said Angel to Jamie.

"Are we in an episode of the *Twilight Zone?*" Jamie said to Angel. "Wow."

Angel was shocked at what she heard. Linda being wild in high school? Not Linda. Not strict, overbearing Linda. Linda never talked about her life much, and Angel was very curious about that statement for sure. First, the shock that Linda and John were coming to watch her be on court, and now the fact that Linda had dated Jamie's dad.

When they finally arrived at the game, Angel quickly noticed that the other girls all had their dads as escorts. Maybe she should have asked John. She also noticed that their dresses were gorgeous.

She bought her dress on sale, and at the time, she loved it.

Now she just felt like a big dork, a big ugly dork. She should have bought the blue dress. Maybe she should have asked John. She always made the wrong decisions.

Don't go down your rabbit hole, Angel, she silently told herself.

"Hey, Angel, I love your dress," Angel turned around as she heard the voice of Kristin.

Angel's shoulders tensed up.

Kristin was the prettiest, most popular, smartest, richest girl in school. She was the perfect example of perfect, except for Jennifer.

She was also a cheerleader.

"Hey, Kristin, you look so amazing. Your dress is gorgeous, too!" Angel said. She actually meant every word because it literally was. She looked like a model as if she was on the cover of the magazine *Cover Girl.*

"Yeah, my mom and I went all the way to Hilton Head to buy it. I wanted to wear something different, and you know, different from whatever everyone else was wearing," Kristin said.

Suddenly Angel felt like that little girl on the bus again, when the boy told her how ugly she was. The thing is, Kristin never actually did anything to her directly, it was always just a feeling she got when she was around her. A feeling like she just wasn't good enough. Well, actually she did do one thing, but Kristin didn't know that she knew. One day last week, Angel had walked into the gym locker room during lunch and overheard Kristin talking to some of the other cheerleaders.

"You know Angel was only nominated because of Josh. Josh got everyone to vote for her to be on court. She really isn't that pretty. She is also a foster kid."

"Yeah, we all know that, Kristin. Besides, she won't win. She is pretty but nobody likes her," said one of the girls.

"Let us see your shorts, Kristin," the girls all chanted.

Angel couldn't help but peek around the corner to see what shorts they were talking about. There, on the back of Kristin's shorts, were the words, "For Josh only."

Just as Angel was about to barge in on the conversation, Kristin said, "Don't tell Angel, I don't want to start anything right now. Besides, I've been secretly talking to Josh on the phone at night. I'm working it, trust me, y'all. He is so hot. I would love to throw him down on this mat." Kristin fell on the mat as if she was on top of Angel's Josh, while all the girls laughed hysterically.

"Good luck. See you on the court," Kristin said and brought Angel back into the moment.

Before Angel could respond, Kristin was quickly covered up with an entourage of her family and friends.

Angel stood by herself, feeling like a big, fat, lonely, dork.

"Angel, you looked gorgeous, you are going to win. Those girls will shut up once you win. They are just jealous," said Jamie. "You are finer, curvier, and a total babe. If Josh doesn't know that, know that I know that."

Angel loved Jamie.

"Jamie, what would I do without you?" Angel reached over and gave him a kiss on the cheek.

"All Homecoming Court, please report to the end zone for the presentation of Queen," Angel heard.

"I guess that means us. Let's go," Angel and Jamie made their way down to the field.

As they walked down, Angel suddenly got very nervous. She never got nervous, she had been through a lot of scary stuff, but this was not scary. *Stop, Angel stop, get a hold of yourself.*

You got this, this is everything you have ever wanted from the time you were little, to be included, to be popular, to have a guy like Josh and friends like Jamie.

One by one the court was announced, and Angel could feel herself go down down into her rabbit hole, her safe rabbit hole. The place she went where she was safe from everyone and everything.

"You won, Angel, you won!" Jamie shook Angel. "Angel, you won. Oh my God, you won!"

Angel was brought to reality, what? Did he just say she won? She won? Angel looked at Jamie. She was shaking uncontrollably.

"You won! Go walk to the front," Jamie pushed her forward.

"I can't walk, Jamie. Come with me. Please," Angel said to him. She had to focus, get out of the hole.

She could do this.

Together they walked to the front of the football field, and before she knew it there was a crown on her head, and they were rushing everyone off the field.

The football players ran on the field to start warming up for the second half.

Angel looked for Josh on the field, she couldn't see him among all the players, they all looked the same.

Angel stood on the sidelines and felt the top of her head. Yep, that was a crown. She couldn't believe it, her school voted for her; 2,500 kids and they voted for her.

Angel looked down at her flowers, and there in front of her was Linda and John, and her sisters. They were crying and smiling, well not Jennifer. She had her arms crossed and was just staring at her. Linda and John actually looked happy for her.

John wiped the tears from his face. Linda stood in front of Angel and had a smile from ear to ear.

"Hey loser, you did it. Congrats," Jennifer punched her arm.

"Thank you, thank you guys, thank um, y'all," Angel said to them.

For the first time, Angel felt like maybe she had a family, kind of. She had won a crown, like a princess. It was like she had become Cinderella. A real-life Cinderella.

Maybe God was looking after her? And did she just say the word "y'all?" She couldn't wait to see Josh.

Angel sat in the stands with her family—Linda, John, Jennifer, Becca, and Julie—the rest of the game. She just sat in the stands and for the first time in a really long time, she began to think about the voice that had not heard in a while. She watched the Warriors get killed with a score of 44-0, but she really wasn't paying attention to the score. She was thinking about her life, the people in it, and the voice that she had so often heard in the past.

Restore.

She heard the voice she hadn't heard in a long, long time, or maybe because she never really had took the time to listen.

Hope.

Angel really didn't know what to say, and maybe she really didn't need to say anything. Maybe she was ready to start listening again.

Angel waited outside the locker room for Josh. She thought Josh played well, but she didn't really know football, and tonight really wasn't about football to her. She hoped that he wasn't too upset after the game about the loss.

She looked down at her dress. It was definitely wrinkled from all the hugs she got after she won. She had so many people come up to her and say they voted for her. She didn't care about her wrinkled dress; she was so happy. She was happy for many reasons, and not just for the crown on her head.

Finally, there he was, her Josh. He came out of the locker room, smiling from ear to ear. Josh had grown up since the beginning of the year. He was becoming a man. He had grown two inches and had thickened up in the chest. Although he was still sweaty from the game, to Angel, Josh was the most handsome guy she had ever seen.

"My girl won! I knew you would win," and he gave her the biggest kiss.

"It was because you told everyone to vote for me," Angel said as she held onto Josh as tight as she could.

"No, it wasn't. You are nice to everybody, you are a good person, and you deserve to win. Did you see my mom? She came tonight," Josh asked.

"Yeah, she was one of the very first people to come up to me. I love your mom, she is so good to me," Angel said. "I know the divorce between her and your dad has been tough. She looks good though. She's lost some weight I think."

"Yeah, my mom has had a hard time but honestly I think them not being together has been better for her. She seems happier, but enough about her, Homecoming Queen. Let's go to Godfathers Pizza and meet up with everyone. We can celebrate. Well, maybe not the score of the game, but we can pretend that didn't happen," Josh looked at Angel and gave her a kiss on the forehead.

Angel was so happy; she knew that Josh was something special indeed.

CHAPTER 14

THE BIRTHDAY

JOSH AND ANGEL spent their high school senior year together, they were inseparable. Angel even told him a little bit about her past, not too much though. She didn't want to scare him away. He knew she was from California, and that her mom gave her and her sister up for adoption, but that was it. Angel was fine with him not knowing, she wanted to appear as if she was just as normal and real as everyone else.

They were headed to college in the fall. Josh was going to play baseball. Josh wanted to be a coach; Angel wanted to become a high school science teacher. She also wanted to become Josh's wife, but she kept that to herself. Their lives were just about perfect.

But on her eighteenth birthday, everything changed.

"So what do you want to do for your birthday?" Josh asked as he wrapped his arms around Angel tighter. Angel and Josh were sitting on the couch.

"I don't know, let's go dancing," Angel said, but only because she knew Josh was not going to go dancing. He didn't party, he played ball.

"Okay, uh, yeah, that is exactly what we should do for your eighteenth birthday," Josh said as he kissed her neck.

"Haha, I am just kidding. We don't have to do that, I would rather spend some quality alone time with you somewhere," Angel said and winked at Josh. Josh winked back, and just as he was about to go in for a kiss, the phone rang.

"Angel, it's for you. Don't talk long because Eric is about to call me," said Jennifer. Angel and Jennifer had been getting along much better lately, maybe it's because they both grew up a little, well actually a lot. They both had serious boyfriends, or maybe it was something else. Angel didn't care, she was just glad they were getting along.

"Hello?" Angel said into the phone.

She wrapped the cord around her arm and motioned for Josh to come sit next to her. Josh wrapped his arms around her waist.

"Angel?" Angel heard a voice from the other end of the phone line.

She couldn't quite place it.

"Uh, yeah. Who is this?" Angel replied.

"This is your brother, Doug," he said.

Angel's mouth dropped.

Josh saw a change in her face, "What's wrong?" he mouthed.

Angel shushed him with her finger. "Doug? My brother Doug?" she said quietly on the phone.

"You want pork chops or applesauce?" the guy on the other end of the phone asked. Angel had not heard that phrase in a very long time. It was definitely her brother.

He sounded older, much older, but he was her older brother.

"Oh my God, it is you. Where are you? Where have you been? Is this really happening?" Angel said.

Angel hollered for her sister Becca to come down from upstairs.

"Becca, come down here. Get down here. Hurry!"

Becca came running down, and Angel handed her the phone.

"You aren't going to believe it. It's Doug,"

Angel looked at Becca and tried really hard to stay focused. *Breathe, don't go down the rabbit hole,* she told herself. She hadn't been down there in a really long time.

Angel and Becca took turns as they spoke to their long-lost brother on the phone. When they hung up the phone over an hour later, Doug promised that he would make arrangements to meet them as soon as he could.

Angel had learned that somehow in the past seven years, Doug had made his way to Tennessee. He said that the Department of Family and Children Services, would not let him contact them until Angel had reached eighteen. Because today was her birthday, they finally gave him their phone number.

Angel also learned that Doug was married and had a little boy. But the biggest shock to Angel was learning about Fammy.

Fammy had remarried again and had given birth to another girl.

Angel just didn't know how to take that.

When the conversation finally ended, Josh and Angel walked outside. Josh had to leave to head to baseball practice. They walked to his car, hand in hand.

"So let me get this straight, your mom, Fannie"

"Fammy, her name is F-A-M-M-Y, F-A-M-M-Y," Angel repeated over and over. "She's Dutch, her real name is Fenncina."

"Okay, whatever, this Fenny lady, just dumped you and Becca, made y'all orphans, never came back for y'all, then went and had another kid with someone new?" Josh picked up his baseball bat.

"That's pretty crappy, don't ya think? I think you deserve way better," Josh said to Angel as he swung his bat at an imaginary ball.

Angel looked at Josh, and thought how much she loves this guy, he always managed to help her sort through her feelings without having to say anything complicated.

He was a simple guy, but full of wisdom.

"So should I meet her? Should I give her the time?" Angel asked Josh for his opinion.

"Babe, you can do what you want. But I doubt that she has changed. People do change, but character always finds a way. I'll support you, no matter what," Josh stopped swinging his bat, and gave Angel a kiss.

"Will you go with me?" Angel crinkled up her nose, expecting Josh to say no.

"I will go with you anywhere, anytime," and wrapped his arms around Angel.

Angel smiled into his eyes; she was so lucky to have him. Her Josh, the guy she wanted to marry.

"I love you, Josh," Angel said.

"Ditto," said Josh.

Josh held Angel's hand and tapped one tap for the word "I," four taps for the word "love," and then three taps for the word "you."

Angel tapped back five, which meant ditto.

It was their thing; they had done it since they first fell in love and since they saw the movie "Ghost" together. Demi Moore and Patrick Swayze used the word "ditto." Angel and Josh had started to use it as a way for Angel and Josh to communicate when Josh was on the field. He would hold up each finger to let her know he was thinking about her. She loved their small inside jokes.

Angel said goodbye to Josh and watched him drive away, and then she walked back inside her foster home.

"So, how did the conversation go?" Linda asked Angel. Linda had stayed in the bedroom to let the girls have some privacy when their were talking to their brother.

Linda was starting supper for the girls. She was making Angel's favorite birthday dish, pork chops, and potatoes. Angel loved it. It had saltine crackers, milk, potatoes, onions, and pork chops. Angel never really got into the fried southern culture, but she loved this dish. Linda always made the girls their favorite dish for their birthdays.

"Well, she has another daughter. I am not real sure about that. Like she couldn't take care of me and Becca, but she went and had another kid?" Angel said to Linda.

Linda got out a casserole dish.

"You know sometimes you just can't understand people, no matter what you do," Linda said as she buttered the dish.

Angel nodded her head.

She just didn't know how to understand Fammy. Angel wasn't a mother and hoped she wasn't one for a long time, but she didn't believe she would ever leave her kids and then turn around and have another one.

"When you found out you couldn't have kids, what made you decide to adopt?" Angel said to Linda.

Linda finished buttering the dish and started gathering the potatoes. She put them in a bowl and brought a knife and the bowl over to Angel.

"Start cutting," Linda said.

Angel wondered if she had hurt Linda's feelings. She didn't

mean to; she still had a hard time blurting out things without thinking.

Angel started peeling the potatoes.

"God made me unable to have kids so that he could handpick the ones he wanted me to raise. When I realized that my gift was coming from my biggest burden, I realized I wanted to adopt and keep foster kids," Linda said as she cut up the onions.

Angel nodded her head.

So if Linda couldn't have kids, why would she want to raise a bunch of teenagers? Angel didn't know what to say.

Love.

She heard the voice.

Because I love you.

She looked up to see if Linda had heard the voice, but she was still peeling the onions, so Angel didn't think she had heard it.

Did Linda love Angel like a real daughter?

Angel had grown up a lot over the past years, and with that Angel had realized a lot of things. One, that Linda was trying really hard to understand Angel. Angel was not like any other foster child she had kept. Angel also realized that being part of a family meant that you had to trust people, which was really really hard for Angel.

Angel peeled the potatoes.

"Angel, take the leftover onion and get the rest of the lettuce out of the fridge. Throw it outside to those rabbits that keep coming after the plants in the evening. I'll finish up the casserole," Linda took the potatoes out of Angel's hand.

Angel got up and went to the fridge that was loaded with food. She got out the lettuce and walked outside to throw the food outside to the rabbits.

Angel walked down the back porch steps. She realized she

had forgotten the leftover onion stalks. She walked back up

the steps and opened the door. When she did, she overheard

Linda talking to herself,

"I heard you, I do love her. She has been a tough one, but

I know she will do something grand with her life. Thank you

for giving me her. I love her so much," Linda said out loud.

Angel formed a small smile. *Linda loved her?* She turned

to go back and feed the rabbits.

THE BOOK OF ANGEL

CHAPTER 15

MORE THAN ONE ANGEL

"DID YOU GET the test," Josh said?

"Yeah, I went late last night and got it after I got off work. I'm going to take it when I get off the phone," Angel told Josh.

"Okay, I have a game today so let me know as soon as you can. I got to go," Josh quickly said and hung up the phone.

Angel sat on her bed, the same stupid comforter with the purple bunnies. What would she do if she was pregnant? She and Josh were in their junior year of college. Josh was playing baseball at a D1 College and hoping to play some sort of professional baseball. His mom and dad had remarried to new people, and Angel was still living with Linda and John. Angel was attending community college and working every evening to pay for her school. She didn't have any extra money to take care of a baby.

Things were better with Linda and John; they were all getting along pretty well. Angel had grown to love Linda and John, and she thought that they loved her too. Angel worked two jobs and went to school but still lived at home. She was studying to be a teacher. Angel knew Josh loved her, but having a baby right now was the last thing they needed. Angel couldn't tell Linda that she was pregnant. She couldn't stand the thought of having to see the disappointment on her face.

Angel walked into the bathroom and took the test. She was shaking so bad, that she had to hold the test with two hands. None of the girls were in the house.

Please God, do not let this be positive, Angel thought. She knew now that there was a God, he had helped her so many times before.

He was the voice in her head, in her gut. She had finally figured that out.

She knew that now, she really needed a negative. She looked at the clock, this was the longest five minutes of her life.

Funny how moments of time flash by your eyes. Angel could remember times in her life when she wanted something to last longer than five minutes. Like the time Linda and John took them all on a family vacation to Nashville. Angel had never experienced that before and she could still remember when she got to hold the baby bunnies. They were so little.

To Angel it was the first time she felt really part of the family. John bought them all kinds of food in Nashville. It was one of the happiest times of Angel's life.

And now she was sitting on the toilet waiting for a pregnancy test to determine the rest of her life. She messed up bad this time.

What she wouldn't do to go back to holding baby bunnies, and not a real baby.

Five minutes was up.

Angel looked at the stick.

She went down the rabbit hole.

Two weeks later, Angel woke up abruptly.

She had overslept.

She had set her clock the night before for 6:00 am, they had to be at the clinic at exactly 7:00 am for the procedure. Angel looked at the clock. It was already 6:30, there is no way they would be able to get downtown on time. The storm from the night before knocked the power out.

Angel dialed Josh's number, "Josh, are you awake? I just woke up; the storm last night made my alarm not go off."

Josh said, "Yeah, mine too. I'm on my way." Josh hung up.

He didn't even tell her he loved her.

Angel scrambled to get ready, she had to wear a dress and bring pads. The nurse said she would be bleeding for a while.

Angel was frantic waiting on Josh, they still had to go by the ATM to get $500. The clinic would only take cash.

Why did it seem like the odds were stacked against them to have this abortion?

Josh arrived, and Angel met him in the driveway. They drove in silence to an ATM to withdraw the money. As Angel approached it, she saw that it wasn't working.

Why was this happening? They were already late, and now even later, and still no money.

Angel walked back to the car and said to Josh, "The ATM is not working, I guess the storm knocked it out too. We are going to be so late."

"Maybe this is a sign that we shouldn't do this?" Josh looked at Angel.

"No, we are going to do this. I can't raise a baby right now and you can't either. You have a shot at baseball. I have to get my degree. Let's go find another ATM," Angel was determined to get this done.

Josh drove further down the road to find another ATM.

"I'll go. Stay here," Josh said.

Angel watched Josh try to put the card in the machine. He put the card in over and over, she knew that that meant. It wasn't working either.

"You are not going to believe this, but this machine is out too." Josh said as he got back into the car.

"Oh my God, what is this?" Angel started crying.

She had a plan; this baby was not in the plan. She was not going to be a pregnant foster kid living on food stamps. No, she was not having this baby. "Just go to the next one," she looked away out the window. She had been through a lot of crap in her life, but today was one of the worst days so far.

Finally after the fourth try, they found an ATM that worked, and got to the clinic half an hour late.

As Josh and Angel pulled up to the clinic, there was a line out the door. The clinic had not opened yet, Angel said a silent thank you, still on track with the plan.

Angel looked at Josh, "You ready?"

Josh looked the other way, "You know we don't have to do this; we can make it. I know we can." Angel didn't respond, she sat in the car waiting for the clinic to open.

At 9:00 the clinic finally opened, and Josh and Angel got out of the car and walked toward the clinic.

As they walk to get in line that had begun to form, two ladies walked up to them.

"Hey, can we talk to you guys?" one of the ladies said.

Josh looked at Angel, and says, "Sure."

Angel glared at Josh, *No, Josh they can't talk to us*, she secretly said in her head. Why is he messing up the plan?

"How long have you guys been together?" The other lady said.

Josh said, "We've been together about three years."

Angel looked down; she couldn't look up. She just couldn't. She had to go through with this.

Don't go down the rabbit hole, Angel told herself. *You can't do that right now.*

"We aren't going to bother you guys, but we just want both of you to know that there are other options and we can help you with those," the ladies said. Angel was trying hard to block them out, she couldn't even look at Josh. "You know that God loves you both, and he loves this baby. Maybe you guys could just think about this for a little bit, and then come back?" the ladies said.

Josh reached over and took Angel's hand. He put his other hand under her chin and lifted her head, so she had to look at his eyes.

Would her baby have Josh's eyes? Angel wondered.

"There is no way we can raise a baby right now. You have baseball, and I have to finish my degree. We can't," Angel said, and she let go of Josh's hand and walked toward the door of the clinic.

She would not look back, and she could feel all three of them staring at her back as she kept walking. She shook her head and kept walking toward the door of the clinic. She could feel Josh behind her, only he was not touching her. She hated this moment.

Angel opened the door, she looked at Josh behind her, and behind him, she saw the women.

She closed her eyes and opened them again.

The women were gone.

Stick to the plan, Angel thought.

She and Josh walked up to the clinic door, but before she opened it, she reached over for Josh's hand and tapped 1-4-3.

Only this time, Josh didn't tap back.

CHAPTER 16

THE DAD

"ANGEL, I FOUND him," Doug said as she answered the phone.

"Found who?" Angel said.

She never heard from her brother. She and her brother were not very close; how could they be? They were now adults, and had grown up in different worlds, different times, even different parents, and different time zones. She lived in Georgia. He lived in Tennessee.

"I found our dad," he said, "I found our biological dad. I found him."

Angel dropped the cell phone. She hadn't had the phone very long, and it was very expensive. She picked it up to make sure she hadn't broken it. She did not have any extra money to replace it for sure.

"Sorry, I dropped this flip phone. What did you say?" Angel tried to resume the conversation.

"I found Steven. Steven Pickett. Our dad," Doug said excitedly like he was completely out of breath.

"Wait, what? You found him? I didn't even know you were looking for him. Are you sure it's him? I didn't even know you knew his real name," Angel shifted to the couch to sit down in her apartment.

"I was going through the white pages in the public library and using this thing called the World Wide Web, which lets you see all the people through a computer. I've been doing it for months now. I always knew his name, you know that. Anyway, I called a few numbers that matched his name, and then boom, it was him," Doug explained.

Angel sat on the couch and listened to Doug explain how he called a dozen numbers and left messages. But she was also remembering the feelings that she had about her dad growing up. Thinking he would be the dad that would one day rescue her from all the crap she had gone through. Now, her brother had found him. She was having a hard time focusing on what he was saying because it was bringing up so many other thoughts about her past.

Don't go down the rabbit hole, Angel. Don't, she thought to herself

"Angel, you listening? He wants to meet us, all of us, you, me, and Becca. He wants to meet us this weekend," Doug said, his voice could barely contain the excitement.

Angel sat up quickly from the couch, which forced her to listen more to what he was saying.

"This weekend? Like this upcoming Saturday? Where?" Angel's thoughts started racing. How would she come up with the money that quickly to take a trip? They barely had enough money to pay the rent and groceries this week. She had just convinced Josh that the cell phone was necessary and they just spent a whole bunch of money on it. She didn't have any money to go somewhere to meet a guy she didn't even know if she wanted to meet.

"He, our dad, Steven, is going to fly from California to

Atlanta. You and Becca can drive up. I'll meet you guys there. It is not a bad drive from Chattanooga to Atlanta. I've been on the phone with him for about an hour. He's been in California the whole time. I can't believe it. I found him, Angel. I found him."

Angel's head was full of thoughts, questions, and confusion.

She just didn't know what to do, her brother was screaming with excitement, and she was pretty confident her sister Becca would be too, but she just didn't know how to handle her emotions and thoughts.

Ask and it shall be given, the voice said.

Okay, yeah, she thought. *Easier said than done,* she told the voice in her head. *I asked like fifteen years ago, and now you are going to give me it? Isn't that ironic?* She told the voice in her head again.

Her brother went on with the conversation. "All right listen, I'm going to call Becca, and then work on a time and place. God, I would love to see you guys, see my nephews too," Doug said.

Angel started to figure out how she would juggle her college classes this week, getting time off from her job.

Would Josh be able to go?

Would they have enough money to go?

Where in the world would she get money to drive to Atlanta, stay in a hotel, food?

They were so broke. She and Josh were scraping pennies to keep things together so they could afford their own apartment. But living in Savannah was not cheap, especially for two young people without college degrees. Maybe the cell phone wasn't a good idea.

Just last night, they went to the grocery store the night before with ten dollars. She bought pancake mix and syrup.

She and Josh just had to survive until payday, which was today, but now this unexpected trip is going to change the budget. She would have to talk with him and see what they could do. Of course, he would support her; he always did. He was her rock, her best friend, and he would want her to go.

"Okay, let me work on things while you work on your end. Just call me with the details as soon as you know," Angel said and hung up the phone.

She still couldn't believe that her brother finally found him, it was still a little unbelievable.

Angel looked at the unfolded clothes that she brought from the apartment laundromat earlier that day.

"I need to fold those before they wrinkle," Angel said out loud. "I'm turning into Linda. Christ, I'm Linda. Geez, what is happening to me?" Angel said out loud again.

She reached into the basket and picked up a baby blue baseball shirt.

She wondered if her newly found dad knew that his daughters ended up in foster care,

Or that he is a grandparent?

"Yeah, he is going to be in for the shock of his life," Angel said out loud again.

Things had been a little rocky for her and Josh since they decided to not have the abortion. Her son was a year old, and he was the love of their life. Josh had quit school so he could get a job to support them. Angel was trying her best to finish school, but with some complications with her kidneys after having Ash, she was having a hard time making progress. Ash was such a good baby, always smiling, never unhappy. After Linda and John got over the initial shock of Angel getting pregnant, they came around. They are now known as Me Maw and Papa, funny how grandkids can change hearts a little.

She and Josh had had some problems, mostly just learning how to navigate being parents so young. When most of their friends were out partying, Josh and Angel were at home trying to take care of their baby and pay bills.

God, was it hard to make enough money to support all of them. Josh's mom had been phenomenal. Angel had leaned on her so much.

"Ash, can you say Momma? Say Mooommma," Angel said to her little bald-headed boy as he used the laundry basket to stand up.

Ash just looked at his Mommy and smiled.

Just then Josh walked in the door, he looked tired. He had been working two straight shifts back-to-back at the chemical plant.

"We're in here, honey" Angel hollered out to Josh.

Josh gave her a kiss on the head, and then picked up his baby boy. "How is my boy today? God, have you gained ten pounds today? You are so big!" Ash smiled at his Daddy and then laughed.

Josh gave Ash another kiss, and turned to Angel and said, "I'm headed to the shower, why don't you come join me?"

Angel looked at her husband. "As soon as I can get this guy to bed, I'll be right up there. You want dinner? I made some delightful scrambled eggs and toast. Sorry, it isn't much but that is what the budget allowed this week. I did manage to make it a gourmet dish by adding some cheddar cheese. How about that?"

Josh laughed and said, "Let me see how I feel after my shower."

"But I need to tell you something. Doug called today," she told Josh.

"Your brother, the one that your crazy mom lives with?

Does she want something? Because every time her name is mentioned it's never good," Josh kept playing with Ash.

"Yeah, him. Only he called with some crazy news," she watched as her husband picked up her son and gave him a kiss on his bald head.

"Say ball. BBaalll, ball. Ash say Ball," Josh said to Ash.

"I almost had him saying Momma today. He almost did it. He isn't going to say BALL, that is too hard of a word. Try Dadda or something, but not BALL," Angel said.

"Anyway, my brother found our bio dad. Like our real Bio Dad. He lives in California," Angel said waiting for Josh's reaction.

"What? You are full of surprises all the time. Your bio dad? Are you sure you are his? You and Becca are total opposites, and your brother well, he just grew up different," Josh said.

This was Josh's way of saying that her family was a little off to him. Josh grew up with a close family, tons of cousins, the perfect Christmas card setting.

"Ball."

Josh and Angel looked at Ash.

"Did he just say ball?" They both said at the same time.

"Ball."

"Oh my God, he said it. He said it! My boy said ball!" Josh picked up Ash. "Good job buddy, you said ball. You are gonna be the best ball player ever, play for the Braves, aren't ya?"

"Anyway, he wants to fly out to Atlanta this weekend, and have all of us meet him there," Angel said knowing Josh was going to panic about money. She held her breath.

"Well, I actually got a bonus coming this week. It isn't much and we could use it to pay a bill but this is more important, so we can go," Josh handed Ash to Angel.

She was expecting Josh to be a little upset, but he was

the opposite. But how in the world could they afford an impromptu visit to Atlanta?

How did she get so lucky?

"We can talk later. I have got to get in the shower. I have got crap all over me."

Angel watched her husband walk upstairs, and she looked at Ash. Ash was rubbing his eyes; he was a tired baby. Angel thought maybe this will be an early night for this kid.

"Are you ready to go to bed buddy?" and she picked up Ash, grabbed his stuffed bunny, and walked upstairs to her husband. She thought the eggs on the counter could wait; they don't cost too much.

Later that weekend, Becca and Angel were anxiously waiting in the airport to meet their dad. Becca was giddy with excitement. Becca was now married and had two small children, which she had brought to the airport. They were all running around the waiting area. Angel had her baby boy Ash in a stroller.

They watched the plane arrive at the terminal through the window of the airport.

Angel's heart skipped, many many times.

Be still and know that I am God.

That's easier for you to say, God. Angel said to herself.

What seemed like hours later, the passengers started coming through the terminal.

"Is that him?" Becca said.

"I don't know," Angel replied.

"Wait, is that him?" Becca asked again, turning her head to look at all the male passengers.

"I don't know," Angel said again.

"Is that…" Becca started again.

"God, shut up Becca. I don't know. I don't know what he looks like, I don't know anymore than you. Just wait. He has got to come through that terminal," Angel said. Becca was getting on her nerves.

"Is that him?" Becca nudged Angel with her elbow.

Angel was about to hit Becca in the back, but when she looked up, she saw him.

It *was* him.

He was short, bald, wore glasses and was with a woman who was also short. Both of them wore white t-shirts. As they got closer, Angel noticed that on the shirt were the words, "We Found Dad" with a picture of himself.

They got closer, and Angel was caught off guard a little. Shouldn't it be, "I found my kids?"

Before she could think on that thought longer, he was there in front of her. Steven Douglas Pickett was standing in front of her.

It was the most awkward moment Angel had ever been in, she didn't know to hug him or shake hands. What does someone do when they first meet their long-lost dad?

"Dad, oh my God. Dad," her brother jumped in front of Angel and wrapped his arms around his father. She watched her father and brother embrace. Then Becca wrapped her arms around him and gave him a hug. Becca was crying, Doug was crying.

Angel felt like the right thing to do was to hug him, but she didn't feel like crying.

She reached out to hug him, and he tried to give her the same hug he had given her brother and sister but Angel froze. She knew he could feel it. She felt like she was about to pass out.

Breathe, Breathe, Angel.

Angel quickly withdrew from the embrace. She needed Josh by her side.

"This is my son, Ash, and my husband, Josh." Angel motioned for her husband to come by her side as she spoke to her dad.

Angel felt Josh put his hand on her back, she felt a little more at ease but she was still unsteady on her feet.

"This is Sheila my wife. She made the shirts, and we have one for everyone, even the little ones," said Steven. Sheila got the shirts out of the bag she was carrying and started to pass them out. Becca and Doug quickly pulled their shirts on over what they were wearing.

"Angel, here is your shirt," said Sheila as she was handing the shirt to Angel.

Angel cringed at the thought that she would have to wear this shirt.

Just then, Doug said, "Hey she can put it on when we get to the hotel, let's get out of everyone's way." Angel looked at her brother. *Some things never change.* Doug was always reading her thoughts, and knew what to say.

She looked at her brother as if to say thank you.

He looked at her back. He knew.

"Well, let's go get your luggage and we can head to the hotel," Josh said as he gathered all of Sheila and Steven's carry-on bags.

Angel was glad the conversation had shifted to them leaving the area. The reunion had caused a scene in the waiting room, as several onlookers had figured out what was going on. She saw an older lady wipe her eyes from crying. Angel wondered if the older lady really knew the entire story if she would be so sympathetic to her long-lost Dad.

Angel held onto the handles of Ash's stroller as tight as

she could. Why was she feeling like this? Didn't she dream about this when she was a little girl? This was nothing like the fairy tale she had dreamed about. She was not going to wear that shirt either. Her brother found him, their dad never even looked for them. Steven, her dad, or whatever she is supposed to call him, didn't deserve the credit. Her brother did the work.

She couldn't shake the feeling that this guy, Steven—the guy that they are now calling Dad—wasn't everything that they thought he was supposed to be.

They walked through the airport. Becca and Doug were walking arm and arm with Steven. Josh was navigating through the crowds.

Even though Angel was walking through the airport, Angel's steps were out of habit. Angel had escaped into her rabbit hole where the darkness allowed her to block out the sounds of the airport and the sounds of her family around her.

CHAPTER 17
THE INTERVIEW

SHE COULD DO this; Angel knew she could do it. She had the degree, and now all she needed to do was land this job. She had always wanted to be a teacher, and for the past two years, she had worked to finish her master's in education. Ash was already in second grade, so this was a perfect time for her to start her career.

She just pulled into the school parking lot, and looked at her watch, her interview was at 10:00 am.

Her phone rang. It was Josh.

"Hello?" said Angel.

"I was just calling to wish you luck. I love you and I know you are going to do well."

"I am so nervous, say a prayer. I want this so bad, so we can start looking for a house to buy, and I can start my career," Angel told Josh.

"Well, if you don't get it, we have been through worse times than these, I think."

Angel laughed because once again, Josh quoted a line from one of their favorite movies, *Overboard*. Goldie Hawn's character had amnesia and couldn't remember anything. So whenever Angel and Josh would get into difficult situations, they always said that line to each other. It was their thing. They had formed a lot of things over the years.

"Okay, 1-4-3 . I'm headed in. I'll call you as soon as it is over." Angel hung up the phone.

She walked into the school building, told the receptionist she was there for an interview, and sat down.

She looked down at her dress.

Why did she wear a dress? She never wears a dress. She looked so ugly in a dress. It made her look taller than what she actually was. *Stupid Angel*, she told herself.

Don't panic, don't go down the rabbit hole, Angel told herself. *You got this, stay focused.*

"Mrs. Parks? Mrs. Rogers is ready to see you now," said the receptionist.

Angel got up and walked into the room, the whole time telling herself to stay focused, no rabbit holes.

She thought that her interview would be just her and the principal, but it turned out there were two more teachers in the room: one really young teacher and another teacher that looked like she had some years of experience, and was definitely intimidating.

Angel got even more nervous.

"Have a seat. Mrs. Parks, this is Mrs. Segars, and Mrs. Lovejoy, they are teachers at our school. They will be the ones conducting the interview," Mrs. Rogers motioned for Angel to sit down.

Angel took a seat, and before she could even sit down, Mrs. Lovejoy asked a question. "Why do you want to teach?"

Angel stared at Mrs. Lovejoy. She scrambled to find the perfect answer, but instead answered in staggered phrases.

"Um, well, um, I um, think that all kids, especially teen-agers are looking for acceptance, understanding, and meaning in their life. Gosh, honestly, I think even adults are still trying to find that out too. But I also think that certain people are given experiences that can help other people, like high school-ers, navigate through all of that. I love science, but I love kids more. I have some crazy experiences that I believe would help me connect with some of them, and I know that being a teacher is what I am supposed to be doing."

Mrs. Lovejoy gave Angel a weird look.

All your life, I have been there.

Angel heard the voice.

She was supposed to say more, what was she supposed to say.

You are called for a purpose.

Angel started to panic. *Breathe. Don't go down the rabbit hole.*

I have plans for you to prosper.

Angel looked at the committee of teachers and opened her mouth. Maybe her big mouth would actually help her this time.

"I was actually raised in a foster home, and that has given me a different perspective, especially one that I can bring to the classroom. All students deserve to be loved, wanted, and feel valued. I know what it is like to not feel that way. If I were given this job, I would try really hard to love my kids and maybe reach some students that other teachers might not be able to," Angel blurted out.

She said it. There was no turning back now. They now know she was a former foster kid.

She held her breath and waited for a response.

They were either going to think she was an idiot and looking for the sympathy vote or maybe they would think she would be a good fit.

Angel just sat there in the silence.

Mrs. Lovejoy looked at Angel, and said, "Yeah, you'll do."

Twenty minutes later, Angel left the interview. She was a little impressed with herself. She listened to her gut, she embraced her life story and used it to show that she could become a great teacher. She had to call Josh.

CHAPTER 18

THE VELVETEEN RABBIT

"MRS. PARKS, WHY YOU reading that book to us? That's a baby book. Ain't nobody got time for that," Chase blurted out as Angel sat on the stool in front of the class.

Angel looked at her class, and said, "Because I am the teacher, and it is my classroom and I want you guys to listen to this story."

Angel heard the grunts and sighs from her class. Every year it became harder and harder to reach these kids. They just didn't want to listen to anything she said lately. So, she decided to share a story with her kids today, hoping that when they left her class for summer vacation, they might take some of it back with them.

"Okay, y'all settle down. I want to read this story because it is a book that means a lot to me. It is called *The Velveteen Rabbit*."

"Like I said, a baby book. Mrs. P has gotten all baby on us!" said Chase, as he was hoping to get a response from the class.

"Shut up, y'all, and listen," Angel heard Randall from the back of the room.

Randall was one of her favorite students. Angel loved Randall not because he was smart or a popular kid, but because she and Randall had something in common.

Randall came from a very poor home and often acted out in class. A couple of months ago during one of the coldest winters that north Georgia had experienced, Angel and Randall had made a connection.

It happened one day as Angel was walking to the front office to check her box. She saw Randall in the principal's office. Angel walked into the office to ask what Randall had done.

"So why is Randall in here?" Angel asked the secretary.

"Yeah, he stole some kid's jacket. He literally wore it to school every day just to taunt the kid he stole it from. I think he was bullying him or something. I told the principal what that boy did. He will be here in a minute," said the secretary as she was typing the morning's absentee list.

Angel saw the jacket on the table in the administrative conference room. Randall didn't steal that jacket. Angel knew Randall didn't steal it because the jacket had been discarded in the hallway unclaimed for weeks. Randall didn't own a jacket, his clothes were old, and his shoes had holes. His hair was dirty and unkept. But Randall was not a thief.

Randall was a boy that needed a jacket because he was cold. Angel knew from her own experience that Randall saw an opportunity to own a coat that no one wanted. So Angel marched right into her principal's office and made things right. She'd even let the secretary have a piece of her mind for accusing Randall of something that wasn't true.

Angel smiled at Randall in the back of her class and began her speech.

"The book is about a rabbit that wants so badly to become real. He doesn't understand that everything he goes through in his life is actually part of this process of becoming real, becoming a real rabbit. There is a quote in the book that reminds me of myself. 'Generally, by the time you are Real, most of your hair has been loved off, and your eyes drop out, and you get loose in the joints and very shabby. But these things don't matter at all, because once you are Real, you can't be ugly, except to people who don't understand.' That's me." Angel looked around at her class.

"Growing up in foster care taught me a lot of things, but what taught me the most were the things I went through in different times of my life. I had to go through those things to become the person I am today, the teacher I am today. I had to learn that some things just suck, but they can teach you how to survive, how to become stronger. I once had a teacher tell me I had a gift of determination and resilience. You all need to know that every one of you can also have that gift. You can always become something, it might not be grand or beautiful, but you can always become something special. Being real is allowing those things to shape you, it is what makes you shabby, which is really all the love that people give you"

The entire class was silent, even Chase, who never shut up.

Angel looked around the room and knew that she didn't teach an ounce of science that day, but that was okay. Her mentor teacher, Mrs. Lovejoy, had taught Angel so much over the past seven years. She learned that it's great to have plans but learning to have faith in the process and people is more important. When Mrs. Lovejoy lost her oldest son to a car accident, Angel wondered how God could take away a child from a mother. Mrs. Lovejoy told Angel that you can pray every day for your kids, but when it is their time, it is their time. You have to have enough faith to know that God will carry you through.

"So, I just wanted to let you guys know how much I love

you, and if you need anything, I am here," and the bell rang.

Angel watched every single student walk out of her class-

room and hoped that each one of them was safe, but she

knew different. Every one of them had their secrets and their

demons. She would just have to let them know that she was

available if they needed an ear. Just like Mrs. Ready and just

like Miss Rowe. But she definitely wouldn't ask them to draw

a llama.

CHAPTER 19

BECOMING ANGEL

KOBI BARKED AT the rabbit and jolted Angel out of her thoughts. Angel looked down at the text again:

He went peacefully.

Peace.

She heard the voice in her head.

What does that mean?

Does it mean you make amends with people you feel you have done wrong? Or does it mean that you make peace with the life you have been dealt with? Maybe it means both.

Gosh, she still didn't know the answers to all of that and she was fifty.

She and Josh had built a life, and now their kids were young adults, who they loved unconditionally. Her kids were not perfect, and they'd both had their share of heartache and disappointment. There were a few hiccups along the way with her kids, but she thought they'd turned out pretty well. They were kind, compassionate, and tried really hard to do the right thing.

That's all she could ask for, and they were happy.

Angel also knew that she has tried hard to make her own relationships with the people in her life meaningful too. Her relationship with Linda and John was stronger than ever these days. When Jennifer called a few months ago and said John had another heart attack, Angel and Josh drove straight down to be with them in Savannah. Her sisters had become her family, her nephews and nieces didn't even know they were foster sisters. Each Christmas was spent together with lots of love and laughter.

She looked down at her phone and scrolled through her pictures.

Her albums were full of photos of her and her family. Kayaking in the mountains, pictures with her dogs, pictures of her kids, her and Josh, pictures of her with her sisters at the last family wedding of Jennifer's daughter. A beautiful barn wedding.

Angel scrolled through and saw her picture with Jennifer, Becca, Julie, and Linda.

She had never thanked Jennifer for sharing Linda and John with her, it never really occurred to Angel to do that until now.

There was a moment during the wedding where the DJ played the song "I Got All My Sisters with Me." All of them—her, Becca, Jennifer, and Julie—danced their hearts out to that song. All four of them were dancing and laughing, like a moment from a movie. It was a cheesy moment and their kids were all videoing from their expensive phones and laughing.

But they didn't care.

What made it so special was when Linda walked up to the dance floor and started to dance with them. Linda struggled to get on the dance floor and she barely moved, but she was determined to get to the dance floor to be with them.

Angel scrolled at the next picture and saw her and Linda.

It was then that Angel finally saw Linda in that cell phone picture. She wasn't the woman that drove her crazy as a teenager, she was the woman that had dated her friend Jamie's dad, she was a woman that was just trying to do what she was called to do, trying to do right, and trying to be a good mom.

She was like Angel.

She was just a woman, a real woman.

Who in their right mind would voluntarily raise someone else's, kid? And teenagers at that.

What a crazy, mixed-up family they had all become, but a genuine, real family.

They were just like all of those crazy rabbits that had taken over her small farm. All of them running around nonstop, eating everything in sight, and constantly having more babies to make the family bigger.

Just like her foster family and now Angel's little family.

Angel suddenly remembered something she'd tucked away long ago when Fammy died. She had got a random package in the mail months after she received word that her mom had died of ovarian cancer.

She never opened it, because she never wanted anything from Fammy, so she stored it away.

But now she suddenly wanted to look at it.

She got up from the back porch swing and entered the house.

As she walked through the living room, she saw her husband sitting in his recliner.

Her husband of thirty years.

Josh.

He was much older with gray hair and a couple of pounds heavier, but still her Josh, the same man she had fallen in love with so long ago.

She looked on the fireplace mantle and saw a picture of her son Ash and his wife, the other picture she saw her daughter Noelle and her boyfriend.

She looked at Josh again.

She understood what God was doing so long ago. He answered her prayers of long ago for a father. God gave her the father to her kids that she always dreamed about.

Josh was her prince.

He was her hero.

She walked toward Josh, and they locked eyes.

As she passed Josh to head toward her bedroom, he grabbed her arm.

"You alright?" Josh asked. Josh could tell Angel was deep in thought.

"Yeah, I'm alright. Just got some news about Steven, my dad. He passed away," she said to Josh.

Josh looked at Angel, and said, "I'm sorry, you want to talk?"

Angel bent down and kissed her husband and said, "No, I'm good. I'm fine."

Josh turned back toward the TV and said, "You want to watch *Overboard* with me?"

Angel smiled and said, "Yeah, just give me a few minutes," and she turned to walk toward their bedroom.

But something made her turn back to Josh and grab his hand. She tapped, "1-4-3" into his hand.

Josh tapped back with five taps, and he flipped the channels with the remote with his other hand to find a college baseball game to watch.

She still loved her Josh.

She walked into her bedroom and heard Kobi walking behind her. It didn't take her long to get to her bedroom. They had built a small home so long ago, but it was still perfect for Angel. Angel shut the door after Kobi walked in behind her. Angel opened the bottom drawer of her dresser and moved a couple of t-shirts to find what she was looking for.

There, tucked away in the back of the drawer, was a box.

She sat down on the floor and placed the box in her lap.

Just as she was about to open it, the door flung open and there was her daughter.

"Mom, have you seen my basketball shoes?

Angel looked up and said, "Yes, I put them in your closet."

"Okay, thanks mom," and Noelle started to shut the door.

"Noelle?" Angel said.

Noelle opened the door again, "Yeah?"

Angel looked at her and said, "I love you, Scoobie." She had always called her daughter that nickname. It came from her love of the cartoon that Noelle had watched when she was a little girl.

Noelle looked at her mom again, and said, "Ditto, and 5, we have a big game coming up in a few days. When I head back to college tomorrow, I'm headed to the gym early. You know I have to score more than my Bubba ever did, so got to get a good night's sleep. I'm going to bed." Noelle played college basketball, and she was home for the weekend.

"Goodnight, Scoobie," and Noelle shut the door.

Angel always loved that Noelle and Ash had that kind of relationship. Ash was her biggest fan.

He never missed a game.

It reminded her of the relationship that she and her brother had so long ago.

Noelle was a lot like her in some ways.

Angel looked again at the box on her lap and slowly opened it.

She pulled back the white tissue that the object was wrapped in. She removed the tissue and saw what it was.

It was a figurine.

Angel took a deep breath, and felt tears begin to roll down her face.

What she held in her hand was a figurine of an angel. It wasn't an angel that you would see in a fancy department store. It was a figurine that someone would have picked up at a Dollar Store. It was made up of cheap plaster of some sort, but that wasn't why Angel was crying. Because in the arms of the angel was a very small rabbit.

Angel closed her eyes.

It is finished.

She heard the voice and knew exactly who said it.

It was God.

It was the same God that held her hand at night when she was scared and wanted to die.

The same God that followed her through the streets as a homeless person when she and her sister ran away.

The same God that was with her at the orphanage.

The same God that laid it upon her foster mom's heart to take her and her sister.

The same God that was with all the teachers in her life that poured into her.

The same God that brought Josh into her life.

The same God that appeared in the form of two ladies at the clinic.

The same God that gave her Ash and Noelle.

He had always been there, in many forms, and especially with the rabbits.

Those rabbits, thought Angel. All of those times, she thought he wasn't there. He was there.

She took another breath and felt his warmth, grace, and peace.

It was then that Angel knew that her journey to becoming real was just about over. She'd became the mother she had always wanted. She had become the rabbit. Shabby, loose, but so, so loved.

Angel got up and placed the angel on the dresser instead of in the drawer hidden away.

"I'm not going to hide you anymore, Angel," she said as she carefully placed the figurine by a picture of her and Josh, and her kids.

She was done going down rabbit holes. She was finally Real—a real brown shabby, but loved rabbit. She didn't know how long she stared at the angel, but she was brought back into the moment when she heard a voice in the background and that belonged to Josh.

"Angel! I think there's a rabbit on the back porch. He's eating those green things you planted," yelled Josh.

Angel wiped the tears from her face, and yelled back, "Let the rabbit eat them. I'll plant some more. A lot more," said Angel.

Angel walked toward her husband's voice, and through her house that was built with a lot of love, a lot of hope and a lot of strength. Angel's step became more like a skip that had been hidden for a long time. It was a skip that represented so many many things that Angel could finally feel. Just like a rabbit skipping through the acres of land that she and Josh owned, just like the rabbits that had appeared throughout her life, Angel felt it run through her body, her mind and her spirit. She understood God's plan. *"Okay, God. What's next?*

Angel didn't hear anything, but it really didn't matter because she instantly knew that he was already working on something new.

ABOUT THE AUTHOR

Angie Bowen is a current high school science teacher at Banks County High School with over twenty-five years of classroom experience. She earned her BA from Piedmont College in Education, MA at Walden University and EDS from Liberty University. She also works as a correspondent sports editor for MainStreetNews. She has also served as a classroom teacher/ mentor and college/career specialist for Foothills Charter Schools. She is a mother to two wonderful children Justin and Jaycie. She has been married to her high school sweetheart, Tony Bowen for over thirty-two years. She currently lives in Northeast Georgia on a small rural farm.

CPSIA information can be obtained
at www.ICGtesting.com
Printed in the USA
BVHW051401250722
642958BV00003B/200

9 781737 643876